# Jingle Jammies

# Jingle Jammies

Robyn Neeley

TULE
PUBLISHING

# Chapter One

SPENCER CARMICHAEL SLIPPED on his black suit blazer and adjusted his bright red tie, taking a triumphant spin across his office floor.

He maneuvered over to his computer and cranked up the volume to the popular Christmas tune, *The Man with the Bag*, that had become his anthem over the last eight years.

He moved his hands back and forth, pretending to play a trumpet while his hips swayed. This evening had been 365 days in the making and it deserved to be celebrated.

Oh, yes. He picked up the football he'd purchased earlier and spiked it in front of a rectangular, cherry oak table containing the popular Warwick's red velvet gift bags engraved with his signature S.C. label. Reaching inside one of the bags, he pulled out the soft, snow-white flannel, letting the material drop toward the floor.

He continued to hum the tune as he grinned down at his masterpiece. "Hello, lovely."

The must-have Christmas pajamas that soon everyone would be talking about.

As the lead sleepwear designer for a renowned department store, his weeknights spent held up late in his office, surviving off an endless supply of cold pepperoni pizza and countless cups of late-night coffee had paid off. What would soon be unveiled to the world was nothing less than a Christmas spectacular.

His smile grew even wider as he straightened out the matching set to reveal a Douglas fir Christmas tree that started with the footies decorated as colorful presents and completed with a glistening gold star right below the neckline. Not only was his creation soft and warm, but these beauties came with something never done before in the sleepwear industry.

He pressed a small button sewn into the bottom's waistband next to the S.C. Exclusive tag. The pajama tree instantly lit up brighter than the one in Rockefeller Center.

"You did good, Carmichael." He'd spent countless hours with his team on this design.

He didn't have a choice. A lot was riding on it after last year's signature Christmas pajamas had been described as "a bit eccentric and lacking Christmas spirit"—*NYC Style* magazine's words, not his.

While not a complete flop, sales last year had been his worst in seven Christmas seasons. There'd been whispering up and down the halls of Warwick's headquarters that he'd lost his edge.

He had to put a kibosh on those rumors not only to safeguard his reputation, but also because another opportunity had presented itself—something that could change his life forever.

Warwick's was in talks to partner with Accettare, one of the largest fashion houses in Italy, known for their sustainable, eco-friendly couture. As part of the deal, a residency had been set up for one Warwick's designer to live in Milan for a year as a creative director in residence working alongside some of the greatest talents in the industry.

Eight months ago, he'd put his hat in the ring without hesitation. The deal could be finalized any day.

His gaze moved over the pajamas. There were no ifs, ands, or buts. This design needed to be a sensation.

He heard a loud, cheery voice outside his office door. Ah, the one person who could ensure that he, his Christmas pajamas, and the company would have a very merry holiday. He placed the flannel set back in the velvet red bag, giving a gentle tug on the tinsel pipe drawstrings.

"Spencer!" Mandy Warwick Adler, daughter of CEO Roger Warwick, breezed through the doorway in a red sweater with a gingerbread man broken in half on the front and the words *Oh Snap* along the side. Her husband and his former college roommate, Tye Adler, was not far behind, sporting a giant Santa Claus wearing a New York Jets jersey in the center of his white sweater.

Back in the day, a smitten Tye would find every conceivable reason to stop by Warwick's. Spencer finally arranged for Mandy to join them for a happy hour and then conveniently bailed so the two could get to know each other.

The happy couple had just come from the company's annual tacky sweater holiday party. He air-kissed Mandy before giving Tye a fist bump. "Hey, man, you ready for the big game?" he asked the defensive linebacker, although he pretty much knew the answer. The guy was an incredible force on the field.

Tye flashed a toothy grin. "You know it, Spence."

"My baby's going to bring me home some Super Bowl bling in February to match the other ring he gave me last year." She winked, flashing the sparkly diamond on her left ring finger.

Spencer couldn't help but laugh. Another enormous ring on her hand might cause Mandy to tip over. "I don't doubt that he'll deliver." He retrieved the football from the floor and opened his drawer, pulling out a Sharpie. "Hey, do you mind signing this for my nephew? I've got a jersey too."

"Sure." Tye took the football and glided the marker across it.

"Thanks, man. I want to make sure he grows up a Jets fan." He reached for the jersey he'd also purchased earlier. "My brother-in-law keeps outfitting him in Patriots' gear."

Tye shook his head, signing the jersey under his number. "Can't have that."

"So, Spencer, Dad tells me you have something for me. Is it ready?" she asked, smoothing her long, black ponytail.

"I sure do." He'd always appreciated Mandy's directness.

It kept their meetings short and to the point.

Especially when Mandy had an important job to do. Given her notoriety as a social media personality and brand influencer, one well-timed Instagram video of her wearing the light-up Christmas pajamas would be all that was needed for them to become an instant sensation.

All of the prep work had been done weeks ago to take the thousands of online orders that would be rolling in from tonight until Christmas. "Are you ready to be blown away?"

She stretched out her arms, nodding her head fast and furious. "Knock my socks off, Man with the Bag."

That nickname didn't bother him in the slightest. He'd worked hard on his brand to conjure feelings of delight by slipping on a warm, soft S.C. design, sipping hot chocolate by a roaring fire while reading *'Twas the Night Before Christmas*—or whatever holiday thing people did in his pajamas.

He wasn't the "sit at home by a crackling fire and drinking cocoa" kind of guy.

Yet he did play an important role in the season each year, bringing merriment to thousands of households as the man who designed the popular sleepwear shown off in family Christmas photos around the world. "I think you're really going to like what I've designed." He reached for two bags and handed one to Mandy and the other to Tye. "Merry Christmas."

Tye fidgeted with the drawstring on his bag. "Better than last year's pink feathers?"

"Baby . . ." Mandy swiftly elbowed her husband as she narrowed her lashes. "We agreed not to bring that up."

Spencer waved his hand, intercepting Mandy's side-eye. The final sales numbers proved they'd been mediocre. He'd accepted that hard, cold fact months ago. "It's much better than last year." He paused, adding, "And no feathers. I promise."

"Well, I can't wait to get into them." Mandy held the bag close. "And no peeking, Tye. I want it to be a surprise." She grinned. "We're going straight home and getting into them."

"Any chance these are *Star Wars* themed?" Tye asked, making a Jedi lightsaber motion.

Spencer chuckled, shaking his head. "Not this year, bro."

Tye took Mandy's bag, holding both of them. "You know I only do this for you, baby."

"And that's why I love you," Mandy cooed as she wrapped her arms around her husband and sacked him with a kiss.

Spencer shoved his hands in his pockets and looked off to the side. Public displays of affection weren't really his thing. Actually, neither were relationships. It'd been a while since he'd been in one, and that was fine. He turned and grabbed his black wool coat off the back of his chair. The lovebirds could carry on, but he had somewhere important to be.

Now that the light-up pajamas had been placed in Mandy's powerful hands, he could get on with the rest of his evening, which consisted of driving to Brooks Bend, Connecticut, to drop off pajama sets to his mother, father, sister and her family—a tradition he'd started with his first set of S.C. exclusive pajamas eight years ago.

He'd drop off the bags, stay for a glass of his father's homemade eggnog, and then head back to the city for a good night's sleep. He'd need it to catch his predawn flight out of JFK to spend the holidays the way they were meant to be spent—sinking his toes into pure, white sand with a tropical drink in hand. He could feel the bright sun on his face as the ocean waves lapped in front of him. He'd be off the grid for two full weeks.

"Are you headed to the Bahamas again this year, Spencer?"

Mandy's question snapped him out of the flight he'd already taken in his mind. "I've got a big blue ocean just waiting for me to snorkel in."

He picked up the rest of the S.C. gift bags, catching a look of pity behind Mandy's eyes. It wasn't like he wasn't spending any time this Christmas with his family. "I'm driving up to Brooks Bend first." He held the bags up in the air. "Have to give them their Christmas presents."

Mandy pointed out his office window, where the snow had started to fall. "Spencer, just once, wouldn't you enjoy a wintery northeast Christmas snuggled up in your amazing pajamas under a warm wool blanket, watching fluffy white snow fall from the sky without a care in the world?"

He laughed at the classic Christmas greeting card Mandy had verbally painted. "I'm more of a 'wish you were here,' swim trunks, and flip-flops kind of guy." Maybe that sounded pitiful for a thirty-four-year-old man to willingly spend the holidays alone every year, but he didn't give it much thought.

Being unattached suited him. He'd seen the struggle his sister and brother-in-law had deciding which family to spend the holidays with each year. He didn't need that drama.

He walked them out of his office. "Merry Christmas. Good luck in the big game, Tye. I'll see you both in the new year."

"Merry Christmas, Spencer! Keep an eye on your social media tonight." She gave him a big hug and winked. "Your present will come early."

"I'm counting on it." He and everyone at Warwick's would be holding their breaths until Mandy's faithful post.

Spencer hummed merrily as he made his way down the hallway, passing by the long train of festive green garland with shiny red and gold balls that connected the row of cubicles.

After stepping off the elevator, he made his way through the lobby to the entrance.

"There he is. The Man with the Bag." George, the security guard, grinned.

"Santa Claus has nothing on me, George," Spencer joked

back, hoisting up the pajama bags. "Have a merry Christmas."

"You too." The old man opened the door, holding it for Spencer. "Take it easy out there. The snow's starting to stick."

"Thanks. I will." Spencer stepped outside and inhaled the cold, crisp winter air, his phone buzzing inside his coat. It took a few seconds of jostling the red bags to see his mom had video called him.

"Hey, Mom." He paused, bringing the phone to eye level. The woman on the other end was in a gray wig, sporting a red velvet mop hat and wire-rimmed glasses. "Mom? Is that you?" he asked, watching her go to town with a rolling pin.

"Of course it's me, Spencer. I'm making cookies for the Elfcapades. Your dad's holding the phone so I could roll out the dough. I've got to make twelve dozen cookies for tomorrow night's Cookies and Cocoa Crawl. Earl, can you hand me that bowl of reindeer frosting?"

He rolled his eyes. Elfcapades? Cookies and Cocoa Crawl? Did he even want to know what an Elfcapade entailed or what was in reindeer frosting? The place he'd left after high school had a tendency for getting fully into the Christmas spirit. Another reason he wasn't fond of small-town life.

Give him an evening kicking back at his favorite five-star restaurant with a nice steak dinner and glass of Merlot, preparing to enjoy a chocolate dessert that wasn't layered with reindeer frosting.

"I just wanted to call and warn you that the roads might be a little slick. The snow's starting to pick up."

He bit back a grin. The perfect excuse to knock and run was literally falling from the sky. He made his way through the building's adjacent garage to his car. "Don't worry. I'm leaving right now. I should be there in an hour or so."

"Earl, get your fingers out of the icing," his mother scolded his father with a wave of her rolling pin. "Those are for the cookies."

Spencer smirked. His dad could never resist a taste.

"Spencer, take it easy on the roads."

"I will."

"No, seriously," she ordered through the phone. "No speeding, and it's best to take the highway. The back roads through The Vine are usually the first to ice."

He reached his Audi and opened the passenger-side door, placing the bags on the leather seat. "Don't worry about me. I know how to drive in the snow. Save me a cookie, Mrs. Claus. I'll see you soon."

As he made the familiar drive north, he passed the time listening to holiday music while keeping an eye on his phone safely lodged in the car holder his dad had put in his stocking last year.

Though he insisted at the start of every holiday season that his parents spend their money on his sister's twins, his mom always made sure to give him a full stocking that he could open before he left on his trip. It usually contained a bottle of sunscreen.

Guilt pricked at his neck. He gave it a good scratch. It didn't make him a bad son that he didn't spend the holidays with his family. He just wasn't into Christmas.

Maybe that was a little weird, given his livelihood.

As he got closer to Brooks Bend, the snowflakes grew larger, coming down fast onto his windshield. He fiddled with the wipers, peering out the windshield. His parents would understand his heading back to the city.

He'd suggest they get together when he returned from vacation—he could take them out to dinner at Dee Dee's Diner, a Brooks Bend hot spot. Better yet, maybe they could all have a nice post-holiday brunch in Manhattan.

He turned off one exit early. Cutting through the back road—or The Vine, as the locals affectionately called it because of its twists and turns—would shave off time. *What Mom doesn't know won't hurt her.*

He slowed down as his tires forged through the un-plowed road. He'd grown up driving in snow, but since he rarely drove these days outside the city, he was out of practice. He flashed his high beams and maneuvered down the dirt road, barely able to make out two feet in front of him.

His phone dinged.

*Mandy.*

He reached over to the phone mount and swiped the

screen, grinning at Mandy on his screen, her back to the camera.

"Everyone, do I have a special, cozy treat for you tonight," she said behind her shoulder. "Are you ready to see this year's ultimate Warwick's exclusive Christmas pajamas from the Man with the Bag?"

His pulse accelerated. "Yes!" he yelled out loud before sucking in his breath.

"All right. Here we go. One . . . two . . ." She adjusted her long ponytail. "Three." She spun around and threw her arms in the air. "Ta-da!" She pranced around in her pajamas, pulling up a leg to show off a footie. "Holiday festive from head to toe."

Spencer let out his breath as his screen filled up fast with little red hearts from her thousands of viewers. *Mission accomplished.*

"Aren't these just the best?" She reached behind her and picked up a mug. "And as a bonus treat, I've added my Mandy's Candy Cane frozen hot chocolate recipe to my blog. You can enjoy your very own Rockefeller tree and frozen hot chocolate for a quintessential New York City Christmas."

She showed off the huge red mug filled with the iced drink, whipped cream, and a candy cane, bringing it to her lips. "Yum! And that's not even the best part." She set the mug down.

"Tye, baby. Get the lights."

"You got it, sweetheart." Tye popped into the screenshot in his pajamas and gave a quick wave.

The screen went dark, but only for a second. In no time, both Mandy and Tye were lit up.

"This year's must-have jammies!" Mandy clapped her hands. "Aren't they simply spectacular? So, let's all get out our credit cards. It's time to ord—" She stopped and glanced at her husband. "What's that smell?"

*Smell?* Spencer enlarged the video with his fingers. What was she talking about? And why was she scrunching her nose?

The influencer began to shriek, "Baby, you're on fire!"

*Fire?* Spencer's jaw dropped as smoke filled his phone screen.

"No. No. No!" This couldn't be happening. He watched in horror while Mandy doused her husband square in the chest with her frozen hot chocolate. "Tye's okay, everyone," Mandy shouted over her shoulder. "Nothing to worry about. Uh . . . we've got to go. Have a good night." The video suddenly cut off, but the comments kept flying.

Spencer's chest tightened. *Did that just happen?*

Apparently so. The rush of hearts was immediately replaced with red angry faces running up the screen—and that wasn't all. Comments flooded in.

*Pathetic.*

*Worse than last year's pajamas.*

*Man with the Bag ruins Christmas.*

"I ruined Christmas," he deadpanned the last comment, trying to comprehend what just happened. How did his pajamas catch fire? It wasn't possible. They'd passed every fabric regulation and safety test. He snapped out of his fog. "I need to get back to New York this instant."

Not thinking, he hit his brakes, causing the car wheels to immediately slide.

Ice flooded his veins. *Get your foot off the brake!* He gripped the steering wheel, trying to regain control, but it was too late. His car slid sideways, careened off the slippery road, and landed within seconds into a mound of snow.

Heart pounding, breath shaky, he unlatched his hands from the steering wheel, wiggling his fingers. Nothing was broken.

He turned off the engine and gazed over at his phone, expecting it to buzz any minute with a furious Roger Warwick on the other side.

His stomach twisted in a huge knot. Setting the CEO's son-in-law on fire was likely grounds for termination.

"I've got to fix this," Spencer said out loud. His career couldn't end this way. He started the car and shoved the shift into reverse. Spinning tires and a large clunking noise he didn't recognize were the first clues the Audi wasn't going anywhere.

*Well, just terrific.* He'd have to call for help.

Angry little faces filling his screen.

Frustrated, he grabbed the red velvet bags from the passenger seat and rolled down his car window, tossing each pajama bag onto the snow. He picked up his phone and punched in 9-1-1.

*So much for a merry Christmas.*

# Chapter Two

"SO, CHARLIE,"—FRED DOBBS adjusted his safety goggles, hunching underneath the Buick's old hood— "you want to tighten the valve slightly to the right, but gently. Turning it any farther could damage the engine, and we all know that this fine piece of machinery is th—"

"Beating heart of every car." Charlie finished her dad's sentence, smiling over at him. As her father's righthand mechanic for the family-owned auto repair and body shop, she'd repaired this standard leak on a number of old vehicles over the years with zero engine failures, but she'd amuse him.

"That's perfect, Charlie." Her dad tossed her an approving smile, eyes beaming with pride. He stepped back and pulled out the prop rod, shutting the car hood. "I'll wipe down the windows, top off the gas, and drive it over to Dee Dee. She'll be glad to have her vehicle back tonight."

"I'm sure she will." Charlie reached for a brown rag and wiped the auto grease from her hands before removing her goggles. Her dad didn't usually offer to drive the cars they repaired back to their owners, let alone wipe down the windows.

She bit down a grin. She—and everyone else in Brooks Bend—could see that Fred Dobbs was smitten with Dee Dee Edwards.

She continued to smile as she watched her father open a fresh-scent air freshener and give the flat, green tree a sniff before hanging it in Dee Dee's car.

Yep. Totally smitten.

She couldn't be happier that he'd taken an interest in the diner owner. It'd been five years since Charlie's mother had passed away after a long battle with cancer. It'd be nice for her dad to find love again.

That was, if he ever actually got up the courage to ask Dee Dee out on a date.

"What's that smile for?" he asked.

"Oh, nothing." She didn't want to push him into anything he might never be ready to do. "I'm sure Dee Dee will be happy to have her car back." She peered out the dirty garage door window. "Looks like the snow stopped."

"How about you join me for dinner?"

She smiled over at her dad. This time of year was always tough on him. It was for her, too, and she went out of her way to make sure they weren't alone, which often meant dinner together at his house or her apartment.

Growing up, this time of year had always been filled with merry and joy—and she still loved everything about the holidays, especially in Brooks Bend. Still, she carried a little sadness around her while doing some of her favorite Christmas traditions. She glanced over at her dad, inspecting Dee Dee's tires. She knew her dad did too.

Maybe they could mix it up tonight. "Tell you what. Why don't I meet you at Dee Dee's Diner? I read on the sidewalk chalkboard sign this morning that White Christmas chili is one of tonight's specials."

After a hearty meal, she'd suggest a walk through the decorative town square. Seeing the bright Christmas lights strung along the shops always lifted their spirits.

"Your mother used to love when it snowed." Her dad came up beside her, peering out. "Said it reminded her of the night she told me she loved me."

Charlie rested her head on her dad's shoulder as they took in the beauty of the pretty, silent night outside the window. No one would ever accuse her father of not being a hopeless romantic.

She'd heard the story a hundred times, how fluffy white snow fell the first time Elizabeth Reinhart had laid eyes on Army Sergeant Fred Dobbs, who was on leave and visiting cousins in Brooks Bend. Three weeks later, before he was deployed, Charlie's mom had chased her dad straight through the town's square on a magical, snowy night to reveal to him in front of a brightly lit Christmas tree what was in her heart.

"Mom used to say that this time of year, I should pay attention to the weather." She laughed. "After I turned sixteen, she practically pushed me out the front door the minute she saw a snowflake fall from the sky."

"You could go now." Her dad squeezed her arm.

"Nice try. The snow has already stopped." She adjusted the strap of her tan overalls over her black knit shirt and entered the office. "Besides, I can't miss all the fun reviewing tomorrow's appointments." December was always one of their busiest months. They routinely reviewed the customer schedule for the next day together before closing up shop.

She picked up the appointment book, and a business card fell out onto the desk.

*Have Charlie call my cell at 8 a.m.* was scribbled on the back.

Hmm. . . Who did she need to call tomorrow morning? She flipped it over to see it was her dad's old friend David Barlow, president of Barlow Automotive Designs.

She poked her head out of the office. "Dad, why do I need to call Mr. Barlow?"

"Oh . . . er . . ." Her dad shut Dee Dee's passenger-side door. "I was going to talk to you about it at dinner."

She tilted her head. "About what?"

"I'm selling the shop, kiddo."

"Yeah, right," she scoffed, flipping the appointment book to tomorrow's full schedule and glanced up. Her dad averted her gaze. "You're not serious, are you?"

"Your mom and I had always planned to sell before she got sick. Now seems like a good time. I've been talking to a couple of brothers in New Haven who might be interested in buying it."

Alarm rocketed through her. "What am I supposed to do?"

"You used to talk about how much you wanted to live in New York City."

"Uh . . ." *Used to* being the operative words. She'd thought about it when she was finishing up college, but a crummy economy when she graduated crushed that dream. She'd gone straight to work for her father. "Dad, that was a long time ago."

"You deserve a chance to go after your dream. Build a career," he insisted. "You sacrificed a lot when your mom was sick. I don't want to hold you back anymore. I know it's rushed, but David has a position."

She put her hand up. "Dad, you're not holding me back."

"You said just this past spring that you weren't sure if you wanted to be an auto mechanic all your life and maybe leaving Brooks Bend was something to explore."

She chewed on her bottom lip. She remembered that conversation they'd had at Dee Dee's Diner too. She'd just broken up with her boyfriend and was having a moment of self-reflection.

But it was a fleeting moment.

Plus, her dad wasn't supposed to retire now.

Her father continued, oblivious to the turmoil he'd kicked up inside her, "I ran into David this morning at the bank. He has an entry-level position open for a junior automotive product developer in his interior designs division. He said someone with your experience and knowledge of cars would be easy to train. He's working offsite tomorrow, but you can call his cell in the morning. He'd be happy to fill you in on the position."

*How could this be happening?* She pinched the bridge of her nose and took the card back just as the phone rang. "This conversation is not over," she said to her dad before picking up the phone

"Dobbs Auto Repair and Body Shop."

"Hey, Charlie, it's Sheriff Thompson."

"Hello, Sheriff." When the town's law enforcement called the garage after a snowfall, it usually meant her workday wasn't over. "Everything okay?"

"I've got a stranded motorist off Interstate 95. Two miles down The Vine. I was hoping you and Fred could tow him in."

"How bad is it?" While most people in town knew how to drive safely around these parts this time of year, there was always someone who took the twisty road too fast. Usually an out-of-towner.

"Driver's fine. Looks like he's got a tire blown out and the front bumper is barely hanging on. Left side's pretty dented."

"Okay, I'll be right there." She hung up the phone, reached for her black, puffy coat, and slipped it on.

Her dad entered the office. "Accident?"

"Yeah." She tucked her long, blond hair behind her ears, reached for her black knit cap, and placed it on her head. "But not a serious one. Some fool managed to get himself stuck in a snowbank."

"Tis the season. Let me guess. Tried to take the shortcut through The Vine."

"Yep." Everyone knew the one back road into Brooks Bend was dangerous in snow. It was much safer to take the highway to the town's main entrance.

"You want me to go with you?"

"No. Sheriff Thompson's there. Why don't you go secure us a booth at Dee Dee's and order two hearty dishes of that chili." She held up David Barlow's business card before shoving it into her jacket pocket. "We have some talking to do. I'll tow the car to the garage and meet you there."

They collected their things and headed out of the garage. Charlie stopped in front of the tow truck's front hood where she'd hung a beautiful green wreath with a giant red bow— an extra piece from the first day of Elfcapades, Brook Bend's annual twelve days of Christmas kindness, that included doing good in the community and supporting those in need.

On the first day of Elfcapades, the town had made wreaths to lay on the graves of local men and women who had served the military. It'd been a special moment for her and her father to place one on her grandfather's grave.

Tomorrow night, the auto shop was sponsoring the fifth

day's Cookies and Cocoa Crawl. The Elfcapades was one of the many reasons she loved her quirky little town.

Now her dad wanted her to quit her job and leave Brooks Bend.

And leave him . . .

CHARLIE MADE HER way through the snowy twists and turns up The Vine, consumed with the thought of leaving the place she'd called home for the last twenty-nine years. Even for college, she'd chosen UConn so she could commute and save her parents' money.

She finally pulled the tow truck in front of the sheriff's car, catching the New York license plate on the vehicle lodged in the snowbank.

Yep. An out-of-towner.

One with a fancy German car. She maneuvered the truck and backed it in toward the black Audi and climbed out, grabbing her flashlight from the cabin's door holder where she kept it.

"Evenin', Charlie." Sheriff Thompson met her in front of the truck.

"Hi." She shined her light over several red bags strung along the snow. "Did the driver hit Santa's sleigh?"

That question got a chuckle out of the sheriff. "No, but he's appearing to have a merry meltdown. He keeps apologizing to someone on his phone for ruining Christmas." He lowered his voice. "It's Earl and Olivia Carmichael's son, Spencer."

She lowered her flashlight. *Spencer Carmichael was here?*

She didn't know him, but she knew *of* him. Everyone who lived here had heard of the famous Brooks Bend resident who made the must-have Christmas pajamas. Dee Dee Edwards had even hung a picture of her and Spencer over one of the booths in the diner.

Charlie never quite understood the big hype. There were a lot of successful people from Brooks Bend, and they were only jammies. Give her a comfy, oversized sweatshirt and yoga pants to sleep in any day.

"That's his car?" she asked, flashing her light over the driver's side.

"Yeah, apparently, he's visiting his parents." Sheriff Thompson chuckled, moving his flashlight away from the car. "At least he was trying to. Now, I'm not sure what he's doing."

She followed the sheriff's flashlight, her breath catching at the sight of the sleepwear designer pacing a few feet away with his phone pressed to his ear, deep in conversation.

He was all tall, dark, and ever-so-handsome, bundled up in a black wool coat, a bright-red scarf wrapped around his neck.

Judging by the car he drove, that scarf probably cost more than she spent on a month of groceries at the Chicken

Basket. She placed a hand on her black wool cap her mom had knitted for Charlie for her twentieth birthday. It was forming a small hole on top from years of wearing.

Suddenly, he stopped pacing, raked a hand through his hair, and kicked the snow. Whatever conversation he was having, it wasn't a good one.

"So, Charlie," Sheriff Thompson began. "I received a frantic call before you got here from Mrs. Anderson. Her new kitten has managed to get itself stuck in their Christmas tree. Do you mind if I leave you?"

Leave her with this man who might lose it any minute? She bit her lip. He seemed harmless, and he was practically town royalty. Plus, the man designed Christmas pajamas for a living. It was probably safe for her to be alone with him.

"No problem."

"Good. I'll see you tomorrow for the Cookies and Cocoa Crawl. Myra's been baking her snickerdoodles all day."

"Thank you for hosting one of the stops." Participants would move from home to home, enjoying sweet, sugary deliciousness and Christmas cheer, all to support the Lakeview Nursing Home.

She stood next to her truck, watching the designer continue to pace back and forth.

"You have to believe me," Spencer said into his phone. "The fabric passed all the regulations. There's no way I would have moved this into production if I thought it would malfunction."

He met Charlie's gaze and stopped pacing. "Roger, could you hold on for a second? Hi," he said, his lips turning up slightly.

Charlie's breath hitched as her gaze locked with his. Dark hair, square jaw, full lips, warm smile . . . *wow*.

The picture in Dee Dee's Diner didn't do Spencer Carmichael justice. Maybe there was something to all the town hype, because standing just a few mere feet away was undoubtedly the most handsome man she'd ever laid her eyes on.

And he was smiling at her. Her. Charlie Dobbs. *Cue the snow!*

"Hi," was all she could get out, her heart reaching a record speed.

Awkward silence circled them for a beat. *Charlie. Get a grip. He's just a man. Say something.*

*Anything.*

*Now!*

"Um, I'm here to help you . . . uh . . . get your car out of the snowbank." *Yep, go ahead and state the obvious. Way to go. Real smooth.*

"Do you think this will take long?" he asked. "I really need to get back to the city."

"Right." She pointed to the tire. "Let me take a quick look and assess the damage."

"Thank you." He resumed his phone conversation. "Sorry about that, Roger. The tow lady is looking at my car right now."

Her speeding heart hit the brakes. "Tow lady," she mumbled under her breath. She dropped her gaze to her scuffed tan work boots.

Well, he wasn't wrong, but did he have to say it that way? Clearly, his seeing her for the first time didn't have the same effect it just had on her.

She blew out a cold breath and bent down to examine the tire. *Cancel the snow.*

"I'm going to drive right back to the office. I'll call you when I'm there. Please tell Mandy and Tye that I am so sorry. I will fix this, Roger." He ended his call and came up beside her.

"Rough night?"

"You could say that." He knelt down, his fancy red scarf brushing the snow. "Thank you for coming out here. How bad is it?"

She pointed to the front of his car. "Well, your front tire is shot, and your bumper's barely hanging on."

"Can you tie it with something? I really need to get back to Manhattan as soon as possible."

"Um, yeah." She stood, pointing to her truck. "I'm just going to string it with some Christmas lights, and you'll be good to go."

"No Christmas lights!" He began to gather the red bags around them.

"It was just a joke." She moved toward her truck,

grabbed her chains from the back, and began to hook them to the Audi. Christmas pajama man was seriously lacking in holiday humor.

"Wait. What are you doing?" Spencer said, clutching all the red bags close to his chest.

"I promise I won't put a scratch on it, but I'm going to have to tow your car into the shop. My dad and I can look at it first thing in the morning."

"You can't fix it now?" he asked, his question had a good blend of annoyance and desperation.

"Well, as for your shot tire, I can put your spare on. But your front bumper is falling off, and who knows what damage you did internally. It really should be checked out."

"I just slipped off the road. I doubt my car needs substantial repairs. Audis are known for their durability."

She narrowed her eyes. Typical. She wasn't going to stand here in the frigid night air listening to his mansplaining what she'd been doing all of her adult life. "Don't you know to avoid The Vine in a snowstorm?"

"I didn't think it would be that bad." He blew out a cold breath, shoving his hands in his coat pockets. "Fine. Do what you need to do. This wasn't how I planned on spending my evening."

She blinked. Spending her night towing in the car of the famous Spencer Carmichael wasn't exactly how she planned to spend hers. "I'm really sorry for the inconvenience, but it's for your safety. Do you want me to give you a lift to your parents'? Sheriff Thompson said you were visiting them," she added quickly, to not appear to be all in his business.

"Yeah, okay. It's about two miles down the road." He trudged over to the passenger side of her truck, flung open the door, and hopped in, red bags and all.

There was no need for him to give her directions. Everyone in town knew where Earl and Olivia Carmichael lived. She finished securing his car to her truck, glancing over at her passenger, who was now talking to himself before giving his forehead a good whack with his palm. She tightened the chains. Had he always been this intense?

Since he'd been four or five years ahead of her in high school, she didn't really know. Hopping in, she fastened her seat belt and started the engine, easing down the road.

"So, you're the Man with the Bag," she said.

"Yep," was his only reply.

*All right then.* Apparently, he didn't want to talk. She began to fiddle with her radio.

"How long do you think it will take to fix my car?" Spencer finally asked after a few minutes.

"Probably not long. Although those German vehicles can be a real pain to get all the parts needed." She waved her hand. "But we know a guy in Stamford who can hook us up. I bet we can get them in a few days."

"A few days?" he repeated, his eyebrows crinkling. "Seriously?"

"Well, it is the holiday season. Everyone's getting their

cars ready to hit the road. Maybe a week to be safe."

"A week," he repeated, leaning his head back. "I'm supposed to be on my way to the Bahamas tomorrow morning."

She opened the vents, blasting heat throughout the cabin. That probably explained his meltdown back there. "We could always work on your car while you're away."

"Great," he muttered before turning his head toward the passenger window.

Wow. He was really upset. She couldn't blame him. "Well, if you do decide to stay here, there are worse places to be than Brooks Bend for the holidays." She pulled up to the Carmichaels' three-story Victorian home decorated from ground to roof with bright red and gold Christmas lights.

Sure, not a tropical beach, but who wouldn't want to spend every Christmas moment in the beautifully decorated home?

She'd walk by the Carmichaels' to and from school and would always imagine what it would be like to live in one of the most exquisite homes in town.

A way different picture in her mind than the two-bedroom cottage she'd grown up in a few blocks away from her current cozy, one-bedroom apartment above the Pizza & Pop Shop on Main Street.

"Anything else I can do for you?" she asked, not really knowing why, but it seemed polite, given his mood.

He scoffed, although managing to lift his lips into a smile—a slight one. "If you could add a Christmas miracle to the estimate, that'd be terrific."

She couldn't help but laugh despite herself. "I'll see what I can do."

He opened the door and began to slide out, looking over his shoulder. "Can I call you in the morning?"

Her pulse quickened until she realized what he was really asking. "Yeah, of course." She reached into the cupholder and pulled out a business card with a tiny truck in the right-hand corner. "We open at eight a.m. Give us an hour or so to run a diagnostic and prepare an estimate."

"Thank you." He slid the card into his coat pocket and stepped out of the truck just as Mrs. Carmichael flew out of the house and halfway down the driveway.

"Spencer, are you okay?" she called out, crossing her hands over her chest and rubbing her arms.

"I'm fine, Mother." He gathered the bags, turning to his mom. "Merry Christmas."

Charlie hopped out of the truck to make sure the chains were tight on his car for the remainder of the tow. She gave Mrs. Carmichael a short wave.

"You were speeding, weren't you?" Mrs. Carmichael jabbed her finger into her son's chest.

"No, Mom." He kissed her on the cheek.

Charlie stood in the road, rather enjoying Spencer getting a scolding, before Mrs. Carmichael brought him in for a big bear hug.

Her heart squeezed. She missed her mother's warm embrace.

Just then, Mrs. Carmichael released her son and called out, "Thank you for bringing him home safely, Charlie."

"No problem, Mrs. Carmichael. You both have a good night."

"Thanks again." Spencer pointed a finger in her direction. "Chelsie."

"Charlie," she corrected, shoving her hands in her jacket pockets.

"Thanks for the lift." He pulled out his phone. "Take good care of my car."

"I will." Maybe a supportive smile from a fellow Brooks Bend native might be just what Spencer Carmichael needed to lift his spirits. She gave him one. "We'll be sure to run a diagnostic first th—"

He was already back at it on his phone, pacing back and forth along his parents' long porch.

Her face fell as she headed around her truck back to the driver's side. *Of course, he would brush me off.*

He didn't need my friendly support because she was the forgettable tow lady. Her fingers wrapped around the business card in her pocket, and she pulled it out, staring down at the Barlow logo.

Maybe tonight was a sign it was time to make a big change and not merely help people get on with their lives.

Maybe it was time to do something really spectacular with hers.

# Chapter Three

"**H**E'S VERY WEAK. I think he needs a candy cane injection, stat!"

Spencer cracked open one eyelid to see his niece, Madeline, checking his pulse with two of her tiny fingers, while his nephew, Ben, jammed a toy stethoscope into his stomach. Amused, he guided the medical instrument to his heart, letting the six-year-old twins diagnose him.

Although it wouldn't be a good one. His slippery collision was nothing compared to the nosedive his career took last night, leaving him shattered in pieces.

This was not the year to go to the Bahamas. There would be no relaxing in the warm white sand. Not with his reputation in ruins and his job in peril.

He inhaled a deep, calming breath, more for himself than for his niece and nephew.

He'd tried last night to call an Uber to take him back to Manhattan, but his mom snatched his phone from him and insisted he stay overnight instead of going out again on the icy roads.

There wasn't any use arguing. When his mother made

up her mind, that was that. But now it was morning, and he had a lot to do. First on his list, get back to the city.

He'd have to leave his car in Brooks Bend while it was being fixed, but that was okay. He'd call the auto shop and arrange to pick it up when it was ready.

While he was at it, he owed an apology to the woman who'd pulled his car out of the ditch. Last night wasn't his finest hour.

He sprang up and shouted, "I'm alive," reaching for Madeline with one arm and Ben with the other, bringing both in for a big bear hug, nearly knocking off Ben's glasses.

His niece was wearing his pinkish-brown feather pajamas from last year. At least someone was.

"Uncle Spencer!" Madeline squealed in his arms. "You shouldn't get up so quickly. You could aggravate your orthostatic hypotension."

"Orthostatic hypotension?" he repeated, raising an eyebrow. "What are they teaching you in first grade these days?"

"It's a fancy term for experiencing a head rush." His sister, Kristina, stepped through the doorway holding what looked like a sweater and jeans in her hands.

"Thanks for the explanation, Sis." He rubbed his head. Kristina was a surgeon at Boston Medical.

"Okay, kids." She clapped her hands. "Head to the kitchen. I've made a stack of gingerbread pancakes."

That brought out huge squeals and an immediate loss of interest in their patient as they raced out the door.

"I'm going to have a talk with them about their bedside manner." He swung his legs off the bed and placed his bare feet on the carpet while eyeing the clothes in his sister's hands. "Are those for me?"

"Mom thought you might like to wear something other than your suit." She showed off the sweater, a tacky, dark-blue Christmas garment with a giant snowman sporting a carrot nose and black top hat made of felt. "It's Dad's. Madeline and Ben got it for him last year."

Tacky sweater parties aside, there had to be a dire reason for anyone to wear felt in public.

And yeah, things were pretty bad. He'd had the worst night of the year, but he wasn't going to give up. And that meant getting back to his office. He cracked his neck from side to side, glancing over at the sun's rays shining in between the dark-blue curtains. The roads were surely drivable now. "I think I'm good. Do you think you could give me a lift home this morning?"

"Sure." She smiled and stood, crossing the room to stare at his wall.

He narrowed his eyes. Something was up with his big sister. Kristina Carmichael—now Long—always spoke volumes when she said nothing. Plus, he doubted she had an interest in his old Matchbox Twenty and Blink 182 posters still tacked to the wall. "Everything okay?"

"Yeah, why do you ask?"

"No reason. Is it weird here without Pete?" This fall,

they'd decided on a trial separation. He'd been surprised when Kristina had called him with the news.

"If I said *a little*, I'd be lying. I invited him, but he decided to stay in Boston. He'll have the kids for New Year's." She let out a big sigh, came over to the bed, and sat down. "I guess I just have to get used to our new normal."

Spencer threaded his hands together. He should have realized how difficult this holiday would be on her. Kristina and Pete always spent Christmas in Brooks Bend, even before they had the twins. "I'm sure it will get easier."

"I hope so." She paused, wiping away a stray tear with the back of her hand. "It really hit me today that he wasn't going to be here. I'm trying to be strong for the kids." She lowered her voice. "And so Mom and Dad don't suffocate me with their worry."

"I think that's their job. That and to supply us with Dad's spiked eggnog."

That got a minuscule smile out of his sister. "Sorry. I didn't mean to get all emotional. I can take you back to the city anytime you want." She nodded to the red velvet bags he'd thrown on his old desk last night. "At least we'll have your Christmas pajamas to wear."

He shook his head. "Change of plans. You're all getting gift cards this year."

"We're not wearing your pajamas?"

"Not this Christmas, Sis." He paused, adding sarcastically, "Unless you want the fire department over here."

Kristina's eyes immediately filled up.

His brow crinkled. *Oh, shoot.* The last time he'd made his sister cry, they were teenagers, and he'd told their parents that she was the one who put a dent in their mom's SUV. "What did I say?"

"Nothing." She swiped her fingers underneath her lashes. "It's just that now we're not going to be able to take our annual family photo wearing your pajamas. It's just not Christmas."

An enormous wave of guilt washed over him, recalling the hashtag from last night. Wow, it was true. He *was* ruining Christmas. He placed a hand on her back. "I'm here. That's got to account for something."

She attempted to smile in between sniffs. "But you want me to drive you home today."

He rubbed her back, not responding. He needed to be in New York City. It was the only way to save his career. "I do need to go back to work, but I have to return sometime soon to get my car. Maybe since I'm not going to the Bahamas, I could come down and spend Christmas Day with you all."

"Really?" she asked, her voice full of hope.

"Yeah. I'll be here for Christmas." *And then right back to my office as soon as the gifts are opened.* He left that part out.

"I'd like that." She gave him a big hug, wrapping her arms tight around him.

"Me too." He chuckled, adding, "But you're all still getting gift cards."

"About that—" she started just as his phone rang from the nightstand.

His stomach hardened. Roger. "It's my boss. I need to take this. Save me a gingerbread pancake."

He walked to his window, taking a deep breath before hitting "Accept." The head of Warwick's suddenly appeared on the screen, and he wasn't alone. Spencer gulped. "Hi, Roger. Hi, Mandy."

"Spencer, did we wake you?" Mandy asked, moving in closer.

"No. I was just talking with my sister. Listen, I'm so sorry about the light-up pajamas. It was a horrible idea that *never* should have happened. I'm at my parents' now because the roads were pretty slick, but I'm headed back soon. I should be at the office by noon."

"Spencer, there's no need for you to come in," Roger said.

Uneasiness shot through his veins. *There wasn't?* He crossed the room and sat on the edge of the bed. If he was losing his job, it was fitting it was in the very room where he'd spent countless hours with his colored pencils and sketch pad, dreaming of making it big in Manhattan one day.

His career? A once-in-a-lifetime residency in Italy? Was he kissing both goodbye?

He extended his arm, focusing on the tiny screen. "I've ruined everything, haven't I?"

Roger was the first to speak. "There's no way to sugar-coat this. We've pulled the plug on this year's pajamas."

Spencer's chest caved in from that verbal sucker punch. Deep down, he knew that would be the outcome, but hearing it from the man who'd been his mentor for all these years made the pain unbearable. "I'm so sorry. I understand."

"Spencer, you're like a son to me," Roger started. "It hurts me to share that there's more."

His throat thickened. *Oh, God.* He was being fired. "I know I screwed up."

"We've pulled your pajamas and are giving heavy thought to discontinuing the line."

He placed a hand on his forehead and dragged it down his face, resting his hand over his mouth.

"Believe me, Spencer, this is not the news I wanted to deliver."

"Am I fired?"

Roger shook his head. "No, of course not. You're our top designer. We can reassign you to the summer line."

He'd built his career making Christmas pajamas. It's what he did. It was like breathing.

He glanced over at the red bags. Not anymore.

"Do you need me to do any damage control?" he asked. "Talk to the press? I'll do whatever you need."

"We've got that covered. The crisis communication was pulled in this morning. Mandy's also going to post on Instagram a picture of her and Tye."

"Thank you," he said to Mandy, who'd been uncharacteristically quiet. "I'm so sorry I embarrassed you and disappointed your fans. I'll call Tye a little later on and apologize too."

Mandy brought her screen closer. "Dad, I've been thinking about this all morning, and I've come up with a solution that will jumpstart Spencer's creativity. We don't need to make a formal announcement about the line's discontinuation until after the holidays, correct?"

"Well, no," Roger admitted.

"Perfect. Spencer," she pointed to her ear. "Listen to me carefully. You, my friend, have lost your Christmas spark."

"My Christmas spark?" he repeated, taken aback. He'd lost it? What even was it?

"You've been struggling artistically, and it has shown in your pajama designs. I know all you need is a heavy dose of Christmas to inspire next year's design."

The line forming on Roger's forehead no doubt matched Spencer's.

"We need you to fuel up on Christmas."

He cocked his head. Spark? Fuel? What language was she speaking? "What do you mean exactly by 'fuel up on Christmas'?"

"Totally immerse yourself in the holidays." Mandy wrapped her arms around herself. "Feel Christmas in your bones."

"In my bones?" he repeated. Maybe he should get his

surgeon sister up here to decipher this conversation.

"Yes! In your bones, Spencer." Mandy grew even more animated as she explained her plan. "Go chop down a Douglas fir tree, make a snow angel, get into a snowball fight, string popcorn, sing Christmas carols. Decorate Christmas cookies!"

"Why?"

"I want you to *experience* Christmas." Mandy held up a candy cane. "And not merely research it like you do every year. Go have yourself a merry little Christmas. We'll handle the damage control," Mandy said, then added, "Spencer, this will be good for you."

How could spending time here be good for him? He stared at them both for a few seconds. In the past, his ideas had usually come after the holiday, well into spring. Maybe they were on to something. Christmas infiltrated television and social media. If he did a twenty-four seven deep dive, he could come up with a new idea.

He didn't necessarily need to stay away from Manhattan to do that.

"I get what you're saying," he started. "But I'd also like to start working on a new design immediately. I could give it to you on Christmas Eve."

Mandy shook her head. "Absolutely no—"

"Hold on, Mandy," Roger interrupted, looking a bit brighter. "If a spectacular prototype could be made to show our investors, it might help assure them that we have a plan for next year, and that we're not ready to abandon the S.C. line yet. We could include it in our Christmas Eve message."

"Done." Spencer nodded. "You have my word. I'll have a prototype created and sewn by then."

"Wait! Slow down, you two." Mandy put up her hand. "The goal should be for Spencer to relax and enjoy Christmas, not to turn around a new design by next Friday."

"I can do both," he insisted. His career and reputation were on the line, not to mention the residency in Milan. He flexed his feet, staring into his phone at the two people who trusted him.

The two he'd let down. He wanted to prove to them that he could design a new set of pajamas worthy of the S.C. label.

MANDY GAVE HIM a warm smile. "Okay, but I better not see you at Warwick's. You stay in that adorable town of yours and have a merry little Christmas."

They made plans for Roger to check in with him in a couple of days before ending the call.

He raked a hand through his bedhead. He hated the defeated expression in Roger's eyes. He'd let down his mentor.

It wasn't going to happen again. He stood and clapped his hands. It was time to get busy. To do that, he'd need some tools to begin his creative process. He pulled out one of his old sketchbooks in his desk, flipping through the pages.

There were enough blank ones toward the back to begin coming up with some new designs. He'd head downstairs for breakfast and then hole up in his room doing some research. He had his iPad and sketch kit with him, so he wasn't entirely unplugged.

He went over to his briefcase he'd left on top of the dresser and pulled out a pencil, taking a seat on the edge of the bed. But if he did things his old way, sure, he could come up with a new design, but what if it was just as bad as the others?

With just days, he didn't have the time for bad or mediocre. He needed to hit it out of the park.

His high school art teacher had a great exercise, in which she'd ask the class to write down five images that came to mind before starting a new sketch.

He opened up his sketch pad to a blank page.

Five Christmas images . . .

Something new and exciting . . .

Unique. Fresh spin on an old tradition . . .

He tapped his pencil, staring out into space, his mind completely blank.

Nothing.

"Oh come on, dude," he scolded himself. "You're the Man with the Bag. Christmas is your jam."

Still nothing.

He hopped off the bed. Maybe if he went for a walk, it

would unblock him. The town would surely be decorated. Perhaps he'd come across something that could jump-start his creative process. Get his juices flowing.

Yes, a stroll down Main Street was exactly what he needed.

His gaze landed on the tacky sweater his sister had left on the bed. He reached for it, pulled it over his head, and patted the black felt hat as he walked over to a full-length mirror.

"Times are dire, Frosty. Let's go fuel up on Christmas," he said into the mirror, frowning at his reflection.

# Chapter Four

"'T IS THE SEASON to be jolly. Fa-la-la-la-la-la-la-la-la," Charlie sang merrily while tucked into a cozy booth at Dee Dee's Diner. She picked up the homemade Christmas card she'd just finished, admiring her glue job.

"Tell me why we didn't just buy a few dozen boxes of cards and sink our tushes into comfy leather massages chairs while getting pedicures?" her best friend, Gwen Polaski, asked, sitting across from Charlie.

"Aren't you having fun?" Charlie grabbed a glue stick and turned over the paper square that displayed the cutest little gingerbread men. "These cards are going to be attached to homemade Christmas cookies. I want everything about the presentation to be made with holiday love." She pressed the paper to her lips and then down onto the cardstock. "Voila. Christmas love."

"Cute," Gwen admitted. "But my ten toes dipped into a hot whirlpool basin sounds really nice too."

Charlie grinned over at her best friend, who definitely took one for the team when she'd agreed to meet her bright and early for an arts and crafts session over eggnog waffles.

And Gwen's feet were probably barking on a regular basis. She worked long hours running the popular Belle & Beau boutique next to the Pizza & Pop Shop. Not only was she in need of some pampering, Gwen was missing her boyfriend, Luke, something fierce. Luke was a sergeant in the military and currently stationed overseas.

"How's this weekend sound for a mani-pedi, followed by an afternoon of Christmas shopping?"

Gwen brightened at that suggestion. "I'll make the appointments."

Charlie reached for another piece of holiday paper and her scissors. As the sponsor of tonight's Cookies and Cocoa Crawl, she and her dad had agreed to not only write out a generous check but also pay for the cocoa ingredients and all the paper supplies needed, which included Christmas cards guests would be signing.

And they'd be signing a lot. Cookies for tonight's Elfcapades were not only for guests, but each host was asked to donate three dozen cookies to be delivered to the local nursing home.

Last week, she'd dragged Gwen to a craft store to pick out all the supplies needed to make cards and signage. She smiled at her pink glue gun that had been her mother's. "Here, why don't I cut the paper and you glue?" Charlie handed over the glue gun and a small stack of cards. "It's very therapeutic."

Gwen gave it a good, forceful squirt, resulting in glue all

over. She waved her hands in the air. "Look at that. I've destroyed Christmas."

Charlie laughed and took the failed paper, handing Gwen another. "You haven't destroyed anything."

"Hi, ladies. What's happening here?"

Charlie's back tensed. Speaking of destroying Christmas. The owner of that high-pitched squeal certainly could. She glanced up to see their former high school classmate, Jillian Fairweather, approaching the table.

With her dark, wavy hair and signature red wool coat, Jillian always looked like she belonged on the cover of one of those pungent-perfume-scented fashion magazines.

And her personality was grating, to say the least.

This Christmas season, Jillian hadn't stopped gloating since the mayor's office gave her the high honor to host the final day of Elfcapades. Jillian vowed it would be the best Elfcapades event the town had ever seen.

Leave it to Jillian to make Christmas into a competition.

She'd given up few details on the event other than her crowing around town that attendees should pull out their Christmas couture before the big night. One of several reasons Charlie had decided months ago to skip the last day of Elfcapades. She glanced down at her tan work overalls. Cocktail dresses weren't really her thing.

Small talk wasn't either, but it had to be done to get Jillian to leave. "We're making Christmas cards for tonight's Cookies and Cocoa Crawl," Charlie said, picking up a stack of cards.

Jillian wiggled her nose. "How cute," she said, her tone flatter than Dee Dee's pancakes. "Well, I'm sure they'll look adorable with my famous peppermint bark I'm making for Evan's stop. I hear you'll be saying a few words tonight, Charlie."

Charlie gulped. She'd rather count all the pine needles on the twenty-foot Christmas tree in the town's square than speak to a large crowd, but her dad insisted she be the one to present the sponsor check at the last crawl.

Jillian's mention of her public speaking was all that was needed to wake up the butterflies resting comfortably in her stomach, but *always* on high alert. She nodded politely. "Just a couple of thank-yous."

"I'm sure you'll be great." She scrunched up her nose. "Nothing like that time in high school English class."

Charlie continued to glue, heat traveling up her neck. Of course, Jillian would bring up Charlie's most embarrassing high school moment when she'd stood in front of her tenth-grade classmates to present a book report on *Wuthering Heights*. She'd worked hard on that presentation and had practiced for weeks.

It would have been great, but her nerves got the better of her in the most humiliating way possible, and turning beet red, she'd run out the class door. "I'm really looking forward to presenting the check," she said, doing her best to not show she was petrified.

"Question, Jillian: is peppermint bark really a cookie?" Gwen asked.

"Peppermint bark *is* a cookie," Jillian spat back. The two never got along growing up, and some things never changed.

"Is it?" Gwen wasn't convinced. "Charlie, settle this."

"Well . . ." Charlie could only laugh while refereeing this cookie war. "Technically, it is a candy. I bet Dee Dee could give you a couple of her recipes to turn them into cookies if you'd like."

By the glare Jillian was now bestowing on her, that suggestion was a definite no.

"Or not. I think peppermint bark and cocoa sounds delightful, and I, for one, am looking forward to trying it. Please thank Evan for hosting the final stop."

Evan Hertzberg was the town's mayor, and up until last spring, Charlie's boyfriend. Five months after they broke up, he'd started seeing Jillian.

A pair she was totally fine with seeing around town. Truth was, she and Evan never had much in common. The town's social butterfly was better suited for him.

"I'll be sure to do that." Jillian lifted her chin high in the air, touching a hand to her pearls. "Well, I've got a lot of work to do. I'll see you both tonight."

"Toodles." Gwen rolled her eyes as soon as Jillian left the diner. "I think I'm going to skip the mayor's house on the crawl."

"Oh, no, you're not." Charlie shook her head because

that wasn't happening. "I'm not going over there alone."

"You'll have your dad."

"Not the same. He has a crush on Jillian." Most men in this town did.

Gwen gave one of her notorious dramatic sighs. "Okay, fine." She continued to glue her card. "So, how are things at work? I've been meaning to make an appointment for an oil change."

Charlie picked up her coffee cup and took a sip. Her to-do list as of late was so long, it'd kept her from having the time to call her friend last night with the latest news. "My dad is selling the shop."

Gwen stopped gluing. "Seriously?"

"Yep. He dropped that bomb on me last night. Even talked to one of his old pals who owns an automotive product design firm in New York City about my possibly working there. I called him before you got here. He wants me to come in on Monday for an interview."

Saying it out loud didn't make it any less surreal. Still, she'd had a nice conversation with David, who'd shared that he was looking for someone with automobile experience to round out his team."

"Oh my God!" Gwen waved the glue gun back and forth. "You're moving to New York City."

"I *might* be moving, and why don't I take over the gluing?" She reached for the glue gun, grabbing a card and running adhesive along the four corners. "David is a family friend. I'd be working on one of his teams that creates and tests interior products for luxury cars."

"That's totally up your alley."

Charlie stopped gluing. "No, it's not."

"Sure it is. Remember when you designed that fancy holder that propped up my phone but had that compartment on the side for my lipstick *and* a hook for my keys? That was genius." Her friend swiped a finger under her bright-red lipstick. "Everyone always asks where I got it."

"Making a phone holder out of some scraps lying around the shop doesn't make me a product designer."

Gwen shrugged. "Tomayto, Tomahto."

"I don't know. There's just so much going on at the auto shop these days. Everyone seems to need new winter tires." She reached into her purse, pulled out her yellow notepad, and showed off the full page of tasks with only the first two marked off as done. "I barely have a minute to myself. I shouldn't be adding 'interview for a job' and 'move to New York City' to the list."

Gwen's eyelids lowered. "Moving to New York has been your dream, Charlie!"

"You sound like my father. It was something I wanted to do a long, long time ago." She sighed and placed her to-do list back in her purse. "When push came to shove, I probably would have never gone through with it. This is my home."

"Brooks Bend will still be here. You'll only be forty minutes away. You can come home anytime." Gwen reached over, touched Charlie's arm. "You know I got you in whatever you want to do. Did you ever think that you're just nervous?"

"Maybe."

"I've got the perfect interview outfit. A great collection of business suits arrived this week. I'll set some aside, and you can stop into the boutique and try them on whenever you're free."

"Thank you. You're right. I'm probably just nervous." Charlie sighed. "I can't believe I have to wear a suit."

"I love you, Charlotte Dobbs, but you will *not* be wearing those overalls to your interview."

She tucked her thumbs under her tan suspenders. "I'd miss my uniform."

"You can wear them on the weekends or for Halloween next year."

As they laughed, Charlie gazed up at the picture of Dee Dee and Spencer hanging on the wall. "Now that guy up there. He definitely looked like a New Yorker, all in black. Well, except maybe for his scarf. You should have seen the one he had on last night."

Gwen cocked her head. "You saw Spencer Carmichael?"

"Yeah."

"When?"

Charlie sipped her coffee. "Last night," she repeated.

"Seriously? Here in Brooks Bend?" Gwen's second question was an octave higher.

"He ran his car into a snowbank, and I tow—" She would have finished that sentence if her best friend didn't look like her heart had just gone into A-fib. "Are you okay?"

"I can't believe you talked to *Spencer Carmichael*. I wouldn't dare. He always oozed coolness. What was he like? Is he as cute as he is in that picture?" She slapped her hands on the table, her eyes going super wide. "Oh my God, Charlie. Was it snowing?"

"No, it was not, so don't even get any ideas." For years, Gwen had texted her anytime a local meteorologist reported snowflakes in the area. "It *had* snowed, but there were definitely no snowflakes in the air when I met him."

"Hmm . . . Well, he's certainly handsome. I can't believe you met the Man with the Bag."

"Well, he was a bit bent out of shape." She picked up her glue gun and a piece of paper decorated with miniature candy canes. "Something seemed to have upset him besides his wreck."

"Oh, I bet I know what that was about, and I don't blame him." Gwen reached into her purse and pulled out her phone. "His Christmas pajamas debuted last night all over social media. They caught fire, and by that, I don't mean they took off. They literally started smoking."

Charlie stopped gluing and looked up. "You're kidding."

"Nope." She held up her phone. "The video was taken down, but look at these comments. They're pretty brutal."

Charlie squinted to see the tiny screen. "Man with the

Bag ruins Christmas. Wow. Who knew he had such power to upset a major holiday?"

"Maybe that's why he's in Brooks Bend." Gwen put her phone away. "He's hiding out."

"I doubt it." Charlie placed the lid on the card box. She glanced back up at the picture, Spencer flashing a wide smile similar to the one he'd given her last night that, for some crazy reason, had caused her heart to rev up. "He said he was headed to the Bahamas."

"Too bad. I would have loved to have seen him in the flesh, all grown up." Gwen rested her hand on the table and cupped her chin with her hand. "My brother used to play soccer with him. Spencer was so good at bouncing the ball off his knees. Sometimes he would come over to our house after school, and they'd practice in the backyard for hours. I was way too shy to say a word. I would just stare out my bedroom window down at him."

Charlie would have loved to have seen that. Her friend had never been the "silenced by a cute guy" type.

"He's a real cutie, isn't he, girls?"

Charlie whipped her head to see Dee Dee sporting a wide grin, coffeepot in hand.

"I hadn't noticed."

"Did you both go to school with him?" she asked, filling up Charlie's cup and then Gwen's.

Gwen shook her head. "He was a senior when we were in middle school. Really smart, always made the honor roll, and good at soccer too."

Charlie cocked her head. It appeared that her best friend would win when it came to Spencer Carmichael trivia.

Gwen stopped to ask, "Do you remember him, Charlie?"

"No. Not at all." That was the truth. She hadn't started hanging out with Gwen at her house until sophomore year, when Spencer and his soccer ball were long gone.

"Say, Dee Dee . . ." Gwen started, grinning mischievously. "Charlie saw him in town last night."

"It wasn't in town," Charlie protested. "I was along The Vine, and I was just helping him get on his merry way."

Gwen lifted her brow. "Dee Dee. You wouldn't happen to know if Spencer's still here?"

"As a matter of fact, I do, and you both can see for your own eyes." Dee Dee nodded her head toward the glass window. "He's been strolling up and down Main Street for the last half hour. Not quite sure what he's doing, but I do wish he'd put on a warmer coat or at least button his."

Charlie whipped her head around. Outside was Spencer wearing his long, black coat, his hands jammed into the pockets as he moved past the window. Seconds later he reappeared, going in the opposite direction. She turned back. "He seems to pace a lot."

"Well, he has to be freezing." Dee Dee pointed to the outside. "It's not even ten degrees out there. Wait right here, girls."

"And that's my cue to use the ladies' room." Gwen excused herself while Charlie began to gather her things before sliding on her puffy coat and hat. She needed to get to the auto shop and clock in. Spencer was probably anxious to hear her dad's diagnosis for his car.

Dee Dee returned, holding two light-blue paper cups decorated with white snowflakes. "Charlie, do me a favor and take Spencer some of my homemade cocoa. I poured one for you too. Snow and all." She winked and handed them over.

Charlie eyed the cups now warming her hands, despite the enormous amount of whipped cream Dee Dee had sprayed on top. Of course, Dee Dee knew about her mom's infatuation with snowflakes and true love. The two women had been close friends for many years, and her mom had even worked for Dee Dee as a waitress a while back. "You know, I already met Spencer last night for the first time, and it wasn't snowing."

"I have no idea what you're talking about." Dee Dee feigned innocence, but her smirk was pinned up by guilt.

"Uh-huh." Charlie pressed her lips together and headed for the entrance. Who needed a dating app when she had her dad, Gwen, and Dee Dee? Pushing the glass door open with her back, she caught Spencer walking by.

"You know," she called out. "Sheriff Thompson might cite you for what you're doing."

Spencer turned around, and she stifled a laugh. Somehow an adorable snowman sweater, complete with a long carrot nose and black top hat, wasn't what she'd expected to see a popular designer wearing underneath his coat.

She tightened her grip around the cocoa cups. Not that she'd expected to see him again, other than maybe to pick up his car.

And who cared what he was wearing? She didn't.

"Hi," he greeted her, closing the distance between them, pointing a finger. "Charlie, right?"

She grinned. "Yes. When I'm not being 'tow lady.'"

That got a short laugh in response. "Well, you do your job well. Thank you for pulling me out of the ditch."

"Technically, it was a snowbank."

His lips curled up. "How's my car?"

"My dad should be working on it right now. Give him another thirty minutes or so and then give us a call."

"I'm sorry if I seemed out of sorts last night. I was a little stressed."

*A little.* She lifted her eyebrow because that statement deserved it. Although, his meltdown more than likely could be explained by the disastrous debut of his pj's.

"Okay. Real stressed. You caught me dealing with a bad work situation." He let out a deep sigh. "A terrible one."

"I'm sorry. Are things better?" she asked.

"No." He shook his head. "But they are starting to look up."

Her cheeks began to warm, despite her knowing that their meeting couldn't possibly be what he was referring to.

"Well, good." She glanced down at the snowflake cups. "Oh, Dee Dee asked me to bring you out some hot chocolate to warm you a bit." She laughed, handing one over. "Although, you'll have to make your way through the layers of cold whipped cream first."

"Challenge accepted." He laughed, taking a sip. "Thank you. Dee Dee always took care of me growing up. I spent a lot of time in that diner back in the day, holed up in a booth with my sketch pad for hours. She never kicked me out."

Charlie didn't doubt for a second he was referring to the same booth she'd camped out in earlier with his picture hanging on the wall.

She sipped her cocoa, following his gaze to the diner where its owner and busted matchmaker gave a short wave before scurrying away from the glass window, disappearing through the kitchen doors. "So, what are you doing out here?" Charlie asked. If his career was in shambles, why was he walking up and down the main drag of Brooks Bend in a tacky Christmas sweater?

"Oh. Don't mind me." He waved his hand and took a long sip. "I'm working."

She cocked her head. "Working?"

"Yeah."

"I thought you made Christmas jammies for a living."

"I design Christmas *pajamas*." He seemed to be correcting her, although she was pretty sure they meant the same thing. "And this is my process. I like to take walks. Move my legs." He motioned with both hands. "Really get the blood circulating to unclutter my brain, be one with my thoughts. Breathe in Christmas." He took a deep breath and closed his eyes, tilting his head side to side before lifting it to the blue sky. "Breathe . . . in . . . Christmas."

She shot him over some side-eye that he obviously didn't catch because he was "working." *Okay then.* "I'll just leave you to breathe in Christmas, but around noon, you might want to switch it up and cross the street. If you keep pacing up and down this sidewalk, all you're going to smell is pepperoni pizza once Colin fires up his ovens at the Pizza & Pop Shop."

He began to smile, no doubt having his own memories of Brooks Bend's longest-standing saucy pie place, and darned if his lips curving slowly weren't the cutest. "I'll remember that."

Just then, Gwen came barreling out of the diner, joining them. "I'm sorry to interrupt. Charlie, there's a shipment just delivered that I have to go sign for." She stopped in her tracks and stared at Spencer with mouth open.

"No problem," Charlie said. For someone in such a hurry, her best friend seemed to be cemented in place, and she wasn't saying anything either. Guess grown-up Spencer still could tongue-tie Gwen with his übercoolness. "Oh, Spencer, I'd like you to meet my best friend, Gwen Polaski."

"Nice to meet you." Spencer extended his hand. "Are you, by chance, related to James Polaski?"

"He's my brother." Gwen smiled up at Spencer, who was a good foot and several inches taller than her.

He snapped his fingers. "I remember you. You're Gwennie, his kid sister."

Charlie tilted her head in amusement. "Gwennie?"

Gwen rolled her eyes. "My brother hasn't called me that since I turned off the hot water while he was showering and threatened to keep doing it if he didn't stop. Hi, Spencer. It's good to see you."

"You too. It's been a long time. How's James?"

"He's doing great."

"Does he still live here?"

Gwen shook her head. "He relocated to Colorado five years ago and is enjoying the bachelor life in the Rockies."

"Good for him." He smiled. "We went skiing together a few times in high school. He always liked the snow."

"Still does." Her gaze moved to Charlie, and then she cocked her head. "And how about you, Spencer? You care for it?"

"Care for what?" He took another sip of his hot chocolate. "Snow?"

"Yeah." Gwen nodded while Charlie shot her some serious "stop talking" signals.

"Nah. Not really," Spencer admitted and drank his hot chocolate, oblivious to their nonverbal conversation. "Give me sunshine and a beach any day."

Victorious, Charlie made sure the word "see" was etched

into her smug smirk. "Well, I should go and check on your car."

"Great. I'm going to stay here for a couple of days until it's fixed. Spend some time with my parents."

*He was staying in Brooks Bend?* Charlie pressed her lips together. If Spencer was staying here, that meant she'd see him tonight at Mr. and Mrs. Carmichael's house for the first stop on the Cookies and Cocoa Crawl.

"Hey, would you ladies know where I can shop for some clothes?"

"As a matter of fact,"—Gwen brightened at his question—"I know just the place. The Belle & Beau Boutique has a wonderful men's line, and I happen to be the owner. I'm opening the shop right now."

"Well, lead the way." Spencer hoisted his cup in Charlie's direction. "Thanks for bringing this out to me."

"Anytime." She shrugged. "I mean, anything to get you to stop pacing down Main Street."

He laughed, deep, and, if she weren't mistaken, a little merrily. "Can't stop the creation process, Charlie."

"Right. I'm more of a live and die by my to-do list kind of girl." Amused, she stepped back into the diner, greeted by a smiling Dee Dee.

"Did you have a nice chat?" the diner owner asked, looking all innocent.

"I know what you're doing." Charlie shook her head, pointing to her cup. "And while I appreciate the effort, this does not count as snow."

# Chapter Five

CHARLIE PULLED INTO the Carmichaels' long driveway and shut off the truck lights. It was nearly six p.m., and her dad and Dee Dee were currently making the rounds to all five participating homes, delivering cocoa and special ingredients the hosts had requested.

She reached for her black tote bag and pulled out the notecard with her remarks she'd stuffed in there earlier, trying to hold it still with her shaky fingers. "Good evening, everyone." She launched into her speech, finishing off with a "Thank you again for joining us for tonight's fifth day of Elfcapades. I hope you and your loved ones have the merriest Christmas."

"That's not right." Not everyone celebrated Christmas. She reached for her black Sharpie attached to her clipboard holding the long to-do list. "I hope you and your loved ones have the merriest holiday."

*Perfect.* She reattached her Sharpie to the clipboard and tucked her speech back inside her purse. Four hours from now, she would be slipping into her comfy sweatshirt and yoga pants to snuggle underneath a warm wool blanket with her gray tabby, Jingles, curled up by her side.

She brought down the visor and checked her hair and lipstick. If only she could skip to that portion of the evening.

But she couldn't let the fear take over tonight. Sponsoring the Cookies and Cocoa Crawl was important to her. The Lakeview Nursing Home residents were too. They were surely going to enjoy receiving the cookies and cards when she delivered them tomorrow morning.

She patted her stomach, hoping the butterflies would stay at bay.

She leaned her head back and closed her eyes, breathing deeply. "It's a one-minute speech, not an inauguration. It's all going to be just fine. No one really cares what I have to say," she muttered.

A sudden tap on her glass window caused her to jump, hitting her head on the truck ceiling. Rubbing it, she turned to see Spencer outside, his eyebrows gathered in. Opening her driver's-side door, she tucked a strand of hair behind her ear. "Hi."

"I'm sorry, Charlie. I didn't mean to scare you."

"It's fine." She hopped out and pushed forward the front seat, reaching for the boxes of cards she'd put in the truck's cabin earlier. "Are you out here working?" She couldn't resist teasing him. If he was, at least this time, the man had on a heavy blue parka, hat, and gloves.

He grinned at her question. "Always on the clock, but I'm ready to take a break. A cookie one."

She laughed. "Well, you're certainly at the right place." She still didn't quite understand his method, but his casual smile indicated he was much more relaxed than when she'd interrupted his creative process earlier.

Maybe it had to do with his new threads. Gwen had texted her immediately after he'd left the Belle & Beau to share that not only was the sleepwear designer handsome and charming, but he'd also been generous with his wallet, purchasing a number of items from her men's collection.

"Can I give you a hand?"

"Sure." That would save her an extra trip. She handed him three boxes filled with the homemade Christmas cards and then pulled out a giant red posterboard. "Thank you."

"What's all this for?" he asked as they made their way up the driveway.

She tucked her clipboard underneath her arm and gripped the posterboard from both sides. "I'm asking all of our Cookies and Cocoa crawlers to write season's greeting messages to the residents of the nursing home who will receive the cookies."

"What a great idea. That's really nice."

She nodded as they climbed up to the front porch. "For many of them, it can be a lonely time without family stopping in to visit with them. I'm hoping the cards will bring some cheer." She glanced over at him. "I see you retired the snowman."

"Yeah. Gwennie outfitted me for my short time here," he

said, jostling the boxes.

"Gwennie." She grinned, not doubting for a second that her best friend was just loving the resurface of that nickname. "Did my dad tell you when your car will be done?"

Her father had been still tinkering with the Audi when she left the shop earlier. Spencer had done a number on his front bumper, but it shouldn't take that long to replace it.

"He said he'd call me tomorrow with a timeframe." He looked away, his voice low and dull. "I'm stuck here for the time being."

*Well, don't sound so excited.* "I'm sure your car will be back on the road in no time. I'm sorry you had to cancel your trip."

"Maybe next year." He gave her a half smile and opened the front door. "In the meantime, welcome to Santa's New England vacation home."

She laughed, her eyes widening as the loud, festive sound of holiday instrumental jazz playing and the delicious aroma of sugar and spice greeted her. *Wow. He wasn't kidding.*

She stepped through a small forest of frosted Christmas trees decorating the expansive foyer. Her boots clicked on the shiniest wooden floor she'd ever stepped on. "I feel like I'm walking through a winter wonderland."

"That's because you are. My mom lives for the opportunity to do it up for the holidays, and she loves her Christmas trees." Spencer set the boxes on a round marble table. "Here, let me take this for you." He reached over for her posterboard.

"Thank you."

"Wait until you see what my mom's done with the living room."

She followed Spencer through the foyer. Her mouth opened at the Rockefeller picture coming to life in the Carmichaels' cozy living room, decorated with nutcrackers, red and green candles, red and white accent pillows, snow globes, and poinsettias. The room included a string of green garland and red bows decorating the most exquisite stone fireplace Charlie had ever laid eyes on.

"This room is stunning." Her gaze rested on the beautifully decorated Douglas fir that stretched from the floor to the ceiling and was decked out in red and silver ornament balls and red satin ribbon. A miniature train set circled around it.

Lit up, it was sure to be spectacular, and a far cry from the four-foot one she planned on cutting down this week for her tiny apartment and would decorate with homemade, painted wooden ornaments that would inevitably be assaulted by an unchaperoned Jingles and her two front paws.

Since her mom passed away, trimming her tree had lost its excitement. With each passing year, she waited closer and closer to Christmas to get one. Her dad hadn't put a tree up in five years.

"Can I take your coat, Charlie?"

"Sure." As Spencer stepped closer, she couldn't help but

inhale his delicious, spicy scent, letting it mix in with all the other aromas of Christmas delighting her senses. She slid off her puffy jacket and handed it over, hoping there wasn't any car grease on it. "Thank you."

"I'll be right back."

"I'll just be here, taking in Christmas." Charlie twirled around and stepped closer to the fireplace to admire the row of sparkly framed photos along the mantel. They appeared to be of the Carmichaels dressed in Christmas pj's over the years, no doubt Spencer's.

She did a double take of the framed photos, all taken in the living room. Mr. and Mrs. Carmichael were sitting along the couch with a man and woman she didn't recognize and two small children. Spencer wasn't in any of them.

Well, that made sense, if he never came home for Christmas. She paused at the last one; a giggle escaped her lips. The family looked like they were about to take fight, literally, in pinkish feathers.

"Charlie! It's so good to see you." Olivia Carmichael came into the room carrying an easel and looking adorable in a velvet red dress Charlie was pretty sure had been on one of Gwen's mannequins last week at the Belle & Beau. Her shoulder-length, blond hair was pulled back by a black-velvet headband.

"Hi, Mrs. Carmichael. I was just admiring all of your decorations. Your tree is beautiful."

"Oh, please call me Olivia," she said as Spencer joined

them. "It's much better when it's lit up. Spencer, be a dear, and plug in the lights."

That request got a big frown from her son and no movement whatsoever. "I think they're better off."

"Nonsense." His mom gave him a pat, nudging him toward the tree. "Stop clowning around. Go plug them in."

"Fine." He moved over to the wall and bent down, looking like he'd rather stick his finger in the socket.

"Thank you, Son," Olivia said, all pleased, and hoisted up the easel. "Now, Charlie. I thought we'd set this up in the foyer. That way, everyone can sign a card as they come in. They can use the round marble table. My daughter, Kristina, will be taking coats."

"Sounds like a plan, Mrs. Carm . . . Olivia," she corrected herself. Charlie began to follow the Carmichael matriarch into the foyer, glancing behind her shoulder just as Spencer pulled out one of the light strings on the tree and muttered to himself.

She couldn't help but smirk. Definitely could add *odd* after Gwen's *handsome* and *charming*. But in a cute, kind of quirky, way. She jerked her head back and followed his mom into the foyer.

She most certainly needed to stop thinking about Spencer Carmichael's attributes. A New Yorker who was forced by Mother Nature to spend time in Brooks Bend would never be someone she'd be interested in. Didn't matter how handsome he was or that her beating heart was a little more noticeable when he was around.

No. What she wanted was to meet someone one day who wanted to be here for Christmas as much as she did.

"I'm just finishing up decorating the last batch of cookies before the guests arrive. Holler if you need anything." Olivia twisted her neck toward the living room. "Spencer, I need some help in the kitchen." She winked. "Wait until you taste Earl's cocoa. Everyone's going to love it."

"I'm sure they will." Grabbing the red posterboard, Charlie set it on the easel and began taping cards to it. As guests arrived, she'd ask them to pick a card from the easel and write out a short holiday message. Then she'd transport the board and cards to the next stop in case any new crawlers joined in.

She began to hum "It's Beginning to Look A lot Like Christmas," while admiring all the cards.

"She looks like an elf."

She glanced to the side, seeing little tots about three feet tall staring up at her in wonder. She removed the hair she'd tucked behind her ear and tugged on her green sweater. Her mom had helped her knit it one year.

"I think she looks like a princess." The little girl came up to her. "Can you make it snow?"

Charlie laughed. She knew exactly which princess the child was referring to. Must be the blond hair and all the big wavy curls she'd spent an hour in her bedroom mirror perfecting. "Not tonight."

"What are you doing?" the little boy asked, inching closer, but still looking skeptical. These were the kids in the family photos.

"We're going to sign some Christmas cards." She handed two to the kids along with a handful of colored Sharpies. "Would you like to be my first two signers?"

The children beamed and sat down on the floor, going to work on their cards.

"I'm Madeline, and this my brother, Ben. We're twins," said the girl, uncapping a green Sharpie. "I'm going to draw a Christmas tree in mine."

"It's nice to meet you both." Charlie bent down and slipped a few envelopes underneath their cards. The last thing she needed was for the kids to "decorate" the Carmichaels' shiny wood floor. "I'm Charlotte, but everyone in Brooks Bend calls me Charlie."

"We're from Boston," Ben interjected, continuing to color. "Can we call you Charlie too?"

Charlie took in his adorable, sweet face. "You sure can."

"It's very nice to make your acquaintance, Charlie." Madeline grinned up at her, sounding super cute and formal.

"I was wondering where my two Santa's helpers disappeared to." A pretty woman with straight brown hair, who Charlie also instantly recognized from the family photos, joined them in the foyer, Spencer right behind her.

He chuckled. "I see you've put my niece and nephew to work. Charlie, this is my sister, Kristina Long. Kristina,

Charlie Dobbs."

Kristina extended her hand. "It's nice to meet you."

"It's nice to meet you too." She shook Kristina's hand, admiring her red cashmere sweater, glittery silver earrings, and black leather miniskirt, feeling a little underdressed in her handknit sweater and jeans, sans any bling.

She'd never acquired a taste for jewelry, working under car hoods in her overalls most days. The exception was the gold "C" necklace her parents had given her one Christmas.

"So, Charlie, you must be the woman who rescued my brother last night?" Kristina asked, her expression looking all sorts of amused.

"Guilty, but it wasn't difficult. His car wasn't really that stuck."

"I would have left him." She gave him a soft punch in his shoulder. "Alone in the cold."

Spencer touched his heart. "Thanks a lot, Sis."

"What? Everyone who grew up here knows not to take The Vine in a snowstorm. Am I right, Charlie?"

"I can't argue with that." Charlie reached for a card out of the box. "Kristina, would you like to sign a Christmas card for a nursing home resident?"

"Of course." Kristina grabbed a Sharpie. "I just love participating in Elfcapades."

"Can I sign one too?" Spencer stepped in front of the easel, examining the cards.

"Um, yeah. Take any one you'd like." Charlie pointed to

the posterboard, suddenly feeling self-conscious. Her arts-and-crafts attempt at holiday cheer greatly paled in comparison to what this real artist could no doubt do. "I know. It's probably cheesy, but I thought the nursing home residents would each like a homemade card to go with their cookies."

"I'm sure they'll love it." He pulled off one of the tiny gingerbread-men cards and reached for a black marker, scribbling a message and handing it to her. "Here."

"Thank you." She chuckled, examining his signature with its big, curvy S and C. "You know, I could turn around and put this on eBay. Make myself a mint."

His expression went flat. "Not this year."

*Oh, geez. Nice going, Charlie.* Way to make him feel awful.

She'd gone on the internet this afternoon and read all about the misfortune that had happened involving a Manhattan social influencer and her popular NFL linebacker husband. The comments hadn't been kind.

"Maybe next year," she offered, threading her hands in front of her. This man who hobnobbed with famous football players didn't need a pep talk from a small-town auto mechanic.

"Yeah, maybe." His gaze suddenly locked on hers for one beat and then another, causing her breath to hitch. "Charlie, what five things come to mind when you think of Christmas?"

*Huh?* Where did that question come from? In addition to

being a horrible public speaker, being quick on the spot wasn't her forte either. "Five things?" she asked.

"Yeah, I say the word *Christmas*, and what immediately pops into your head?"

"Um, Christmas is . . . I think of," she struggled. Just then, the doorbell rang, followed by the first group of attendees singing "Deck the Halls" at the top of their lungs.

"Christmas carols," she said smugly as the foyer filled up with the cheery faces of neighbors, friends, and customers she'd known for years.

"That's cheating, and I'll need four more." Spencer grinned. "I look forward to hearing the rest of your answers to that Christmas quiz later tonight, but right now I have to get back to my cookie-decorating duty."

"Very important duty," she nodded, adding jokingly, "And I will start studying for that quiz."

"Don't study, just what you feel."

*What I feel.* Her cheeks heated as he said a few hellos and disappeared out of the foyer. What she was feeling was a rush of excitement that she needed to temper stat. She turned to greet the guests, ignoring all the heart palpitations that the idea of spending more time tonight with Spencer Carmichael was now causing.

"CHARLIE, I MADE this for you."

Madeline held up a clear Santa mug filled with light-green liquid and topped with green whipped cream covered with tiny red hearts.

"Oh wow. Look at that."

Kristina came up alongside her daughter, resting her hands on Madeline's shoulders. "It's my dad's famous Christmas Grinch hot chocolate." She lowered her voice. "Nothing toxic, just a lot of green food coloring, and my dad adds a healthy shot of peppermint schnapps for the adults."

Charlie took a sip, the warm, sugary mint concoction exploding over her taste buds. "It's delicious." She took another drink. "Really amazing."

"My father pulled out all the stops to take first place in the hot cocoa contest." Kristina pointed to Mr. Carmichael bent over, starting the train set around the tree. "Maddie, go help your grandpa before he throws out his back."

Charlie continued to enjoy her drink. "He just might take it." She stepped closer to the fireplace. "I can't get over how beautiful this is. I've always wanted one."

"A stone fireplace?"

"Any fireplace, really. My parents were more of a 'one space heater in the living room and extra blankets to keep warm' type of family."

Kristina picked up one of the red Christmas pillows and fluffed it. "We've made a lot of wonderful memories in this room over the years."

"I can see that." Charlie sipped her cocoa, glancing at the

photos.

"It's so nice to have my brother home in Brooks Bend. I never get to see him. He's usually sending us a text right about now from the Bahamas."

Charlie stood, feeling a little awkward for asking what she'd been thinking. It wasn't really her business, but she was curious. "I can't understand how someone could not want to spend Christmas in Brooks Bend. I mean, strolling Main Street all decorated on a wintery night or skating on the town's ice rink to live, festive music. Truly. Nothing beats it."

Kristina nodded. "I totally agree. He's missing out."

"Oh, Charlie." Olivia joined the conversation. "Just the woman I was looking for."

*She was?* "What can I do for you?"

"Could you do me a favor and give my son some help in the kitchen? If he doesn't finish decorating the cookies, you won't have our donation before we all crawl over to Sheriff Thompson's place."

Kristina laughed, rolling her eyes. "He's probably being creative. Charlie, fair warning. It's Spencer's process."

"Oh, I've had the privilege of seeing that process play out in action. This morning outside Dee Dee's Diner, in fact." Charlie tugged down her sweater. "Don't you worry, Mrs. Carmichael. I'll give him a heavy dose of Charlie 'Just Get It Done' Dobbs." She excused herself, but not before catching Kristina's "I like her" remark.

Feeling her cheeks flush again, she moved through the room, sidestepping Jillian and Evan holding court near the big bay windows with a polite nod. She said a quick hello to her dad, who was lingering by the living room entrance with Dee Dee, both sipping the green hot chocolate.

"Hey, Dad. I meant to ask earlier. When do you think Spencer's car will be done?"

Her father made eyes with Dee Dee, not saying a word.

"Guys . . .?" She lowered her lashes at the nonverbal conversation happening in front of her. "Is there something I don't know?"

"Nope." Her dad waved her off. "Car should be done in a week, maybe a little longer."

"Longer than a week?"

"I spent some time underneath it this afternoon and realized I need to order a special part. You know how tricky it is to fix foreign automobiles. The simplest thing could take much longer than if it were a Ford or Chevy."

"Uh-huh," she said flatly. She did know a thing or two about Audis and wasn't buying it. "I think I'll take a look in the morning for myself." She passed the foyer and headed down the hallway, admiring both walls decorated with various-shaped pictures wrapped with Christmas wrapping paper.

Stepping into the kitchen, a laugh escaped her at the sight in front of her. Spencer stood behind a long center island with his hands on his hips, glancing intently at a cookie, his black sweater covered in flour. She hung back for a second, watching him grab an icing piping bag off the island and bend down, meticulously going to work.

"Well, what do we have here? A sleepwear designer by day, cookie designer by night, perhaps?"

He glanced up and flashed a wide smile. "Oh, hey."

"Whatcha doin'?" She asked the obvious, but it was a logical question given his intensity.

"Still decorating Christmas cookies." He picked up his snowflake, showing it off. "What do you think?"

She grinned despite the fact that her mother would've interpreted the snowflake as a clear sign. A beautiful one in white and silver icing and decorated with various shades of blue dots around its edges. "Wow. That is something."

He held it high up in the air, inspecting it. "It is, isn't it?"

She stepped closer to the kitchen island, eyeing a whole rack full of sugar cookies to be frosted. "Um, Spencer, how many cookies have you decorated?"

"Two, but the first one didn't count. I changed course halfway through the decoration, so I ate it."

*Only two?* She blocked the laugh about to escape her lips with her two fingers. "It's been more than an hour since your mom asked for help."

"Yeah, but I had to see what I was working with."

"What you were working with?" she repeated, setting down her cocoa and folding her arms. *Oh, boy. This ought to be good.*

He nodded and picked up one of the unfrosted cookies off the rack, tracing its edge with the back of the spoon. "Step one in the Spencer Carmichael decoration process. Examining the cut of the cookie, its shape, and determining its overall sturdiness."

"I see," she played along. "Well, it is true that there would be no greater disaster than a Christmas cookie crumbling before it's frosted."

"Exactly." He picked up the icing piping bag. "Plus, the frosting ratio of white and silver had to be just right to cast a shimmering effect," he said, showing off his cookie again. "See?"

It certainly did sparkle—she'd give him that. "You nailed it, but, Spencer, it's a cookie."

"It's an original S.C. Christmas cookie," he said with a lot of pride in that correction.

"Well, it's a Christmas cookie that's going to be eaten in the next twenty-four hours." She smiled. "Here, let me try." She arranged six cookies in a row and dipped a spatula into the icing. No need for a piping bag. Within three minutes, they were all frosted. She reached for the bowl of sprinkles, and with a spoon, dusted each cookie. "And that's how you get it done."

He grinned. "My decorated cookie would win awards."

"And my decorated *cookies* will be enjoyed by many."

"You may have a point." He reached for an unfrosted

cookie. "However, I'm going to work on replicating this masterpiece while you mass produce."

She couldn't help but chuckle. "I will not stand in the way of your creativity. That is, until it's time to leave for the next house on the crawl, which is really any minute."

"Can't wait." He reached for the piping bag and spooned more white frosting into it. "I've been really missing out all these years."

She continued to sprinkle the cookies. She shouldn't ask. It was really none of her business. But he'd opened the door. "What happened with this year's pj's?" She paused, correcting herself for his benefit. "I mean, pajamas?"

He blew out a breath, a loud one, before going back to work on his masterpiece. "It wasn't good, Charlie. They crashed and burned." He filled in the silver frosting and spread it with a knife. "Well, I guess it was more like they burned all over social media, and then I crashed into a snowbank."

Aww. He was attempting a funny. Maybe that was a good sign. "I saw," she admitted, reaching for an empty cookie tin on the counter and removing the lid.

He glanced up. "You saw the video?"

"No." She shook her head. "I read some of the comments this morning. The video had already been taken down."

"Oh." He went back to his decorating. "You're better off."

She began to stack the cookies inside the tin. When she was all done, she finally broke the silence. "If you don't want to talk about it, I totally understand. But what exactly happened?"

"No, it's not that." He placed his cookie in the tin with the others and turned to the sink, flipping up the faucet and running his hands under. "I'm still trying to figure that out. I don't know. Maybe I should have gone with snowflakes for this year's pajama design. Christmas. Classic. Timeless."

She pressed her lips together and gulped. "Oh, I don't know. The feathers were pretty fun."

He wiped his hand on a dishcloth. "Did you buy a pair?"

"No," she admitted, shaking her head. "I noticed all the family photos above the mantel. In my opinion, birds are an underrepresented part of Christmas."

"They were meant to be three French hens."

"I can totally see that now. That's super creative."

He laughed. "Yeah. It was a unique take on the Third Day of Christmas." He swiped the dishcloth over his sweater, attempting to get off the flour. "I honestly believed they'd be a huge hit, but it turned out, not so much."

"Well, the third day's not as popular as the fifth," she joked, pointing to the cookies.

"Maybe I should do an Elfcapades design." He set the dishcloth off to the side, looking serious. "I need to come up with a prototype for next year's pajamas in the next two weeks."

She stopped filling the container. "Is that what you were trying to do this morning? Think up a new design?"

"I've promised my boss a new design by Christmas Eve to calm investors." He sighed. "However, my creativity seems to be on empty."

"But you're the Man with the Bag. You do this every year."

"And I have months to do it." He grimaced and looked away. "The whole Christmas thing doesn't really come easy to me. I might be the Man with the Bag, but I'm also the guy who normally spends his holidays alone sprawled out on a beach towel with sand between my toes."

She watched as he started to tidy up the kitchen island in silence, her chest growing tight. What an enormous amount of pressure he must be under. Maybe she could give him a Christmas tip or two to inspire him for tomorrow's jaunt up and down Main Street. "So, I've been thinking about the question you asked me earlier."

He grabbed a sponge from the sink and started wiping down the counter. "What's that?"

"The five things that remind me of Christmas. One is definitely walking through the snow to select my Christmas tree at the top of The Vine. It's so beautiful and peaceful up there. Growing up, my mom and I loved getting lost in the maze of trees while searching for the perfect one."

He set the sponge down and put his palms flat on the counter. "What else?"

The intensity of his deep-blue eyes sent tingles skittering up her spine. She placed a hand on her neck. "Well, I never miss ice-skating to loud Christmas music on Brooks Bend's outdoor rink. That's happening tomorrow night for the sixth day of Elfcapades. There's even a Christmas goose involved this year."

"Christmas goose?"

"Uh-huh."

"Really?" He grinned, waggling his eyebrows. "Tell me more."

She found it easy for some reason to share her time-honored Christmas traditions with this stranger. "I always enjoy watching a favorite holiday classic while drinking warm eggnog. Nothing, however, beats strolling down Main Street before the ceremonial lighting of the town's tree while chomping on Christmas tree pizza from the Pizza & Pop Shop."

"Colin still does that?" His grin was wide.

"He sure does. Every single year. It's on Monday. You'll have to come."

"Oh, well, I'll probably be back in New York by then," he said.

Her shoulders slumped. Of course he'd leave. His home wasn't here but miles away. She straightened. "We take a lot of pictures and post on the town's social media pages. You can check them out. Maybe for inspiration."

"I'll be sure to do that." He cocked his head. "What's the

number one thing that reminds you of Christmas?"

"Well . . ." She took a deep breath. It used to be the annual tree-trimming party at her parents', but those were no more.

Three years ago, she'd started a new tradition. "Picking out the perfect book for my mom and reading it on Christmas Eve. That's now my favorite one." She broke his gaze and glanced down at the cookie tin, her heart squeezing.

"These all sound like wonderful traditions. What book are you getting your mom this year?"

She could have told him the truth about this tradition, and she did. Sort of. "I chose a classic. *Pride and Prejudice*."

All of a sudden, loud singing from the foyer indicated that people were leaving for the next house. "I guess we should go join the crawlers."

"Thank you for your help." He chuckled. "You may be onto something with efficiency. Perhaps that's what my process is lacking with such a tight deadline."

"Taskmaster is my middle name," she kidded. "Maybe I should design your pajamas."

That, too, got a laugh—with her, not at her. "Maybe you should. I'll go get our jackets."

Charlie picked up the tin's top, glancing down at the perfect snowflake Spencer had decorated. Was there more to the Man with the Bag?

# Chapter Six

S PENCER HUMMED "JINGLE Bells" as he walked down the moonlit street, looping arms with his sister. They were successfully crawling their way to the fifth and final stop of tonight's cookie extravaganza.

"You're in a jingly mood this evening." Kristina looped her arm in his.

"It's the sugar." He inhaled the cool, crisp night. "Can you smell it? Christmas is in the air."

"Is it inspiring a new idea for your pajama design?"

"Well . . ." He'd filled his sister in that afternoon while they were on a last-minute errand run to the Chicken Basket to pick up sprinkles for his mom's cookies. "My usual process is to let my mind go for a few hours. Really open it up and let Christmas in."

"And?"

"Not a single original idea," he admitted. "Everything I've come up with I've already done before or it isn't all that exciting. I don't know, Sis. Maybe eight designs were all that were in me. Think it's too late for me to go to med school?"

"And rid the world of the opportunity to slip into an exclusive pair of S.C. Christmas jammies?"

"Pajamas." He shook his head. "Why can't I make that stick?"

"Because jammies conjure up an entirely different feeling. Fun and festive." She patted his arm. "I have faith in you. You just need some new inspiration. Change up your process. I bet an idea will come then."

"Yeah, hopefully. I really need to prove I've still got it."

"Maybe your problem is you're hyper-focused and could use a little distraction while you're waiting for inspiration to strike."

*Distraction?* What did she think tonight was? "Crawling with my sister through our small hometown in the dead of winter is definitely distracting me from my work."

"I mean like a date." She pointed to Charlie walking ahead of them a few feet, her wavy blond hair flowing down her back. "A holiday one."

"With who? The auto mechanic?" he asked, taken aback. Sure, he'd admit it. Charlie was certainly cute, and he'd enjoyed their time frosting cookies earlier, but they hadn't really spoke after that. "I don't know if she's really my type. The women I date in New York tend to be . . ."

He searched his memory for the last time he'd been on a date. It'd been a few months ago, over the summer, with a woman he'd met at his gym—an account supervisor for a large insurance firm. Their time together hadn't been all that interesting, and any chemistry between them completely fizzled after three dates. "I like being single."

Just then, Charlie slowed her pace and appeared to be reading an index card. He winked. "But it doesn't mean I can't go spread some Christmas cheer."

"You go do that." Kristina gave him an encouraging nudge forward.

He picked up his steps. Suddenly, an arm slipped into his.

And it wasn't his sister's.

"Spencer Carmichael, I was hoping to get you alone."

He looked down to see Jillian Fairweather's bright-white smile. He hadn't remembered this perky brunette growing up since she, like Charlie and Gwen, had been a few years behind him in school, but that hadn't stopped her from cornering him at the last stop and talking his ear off the entire time they were there. He'd learned that she owned Brooks Buds floral shop on Main Street and was dating the mayor.

Not that he'd inquired about her relationship status. She'd offered up that news all on her own.

He gazed ahead at Charlie, now walking with Gwen. "Um, you were looking for me?" They'd just finished their conversation not fifteen minutes ago. What could she possibly need to speak to him about in that short time?

"Yes. I was talking to some of the girls on our walk. I don't know if you've heard, but I'm planning the twelfth day of Elfcapades."

"I hadn't heard. Let me guess—it involves drummers drumming?"

"Not exactly. It was to be the Jingle Bell Ball, but then you came to town, and I've come up with something way better than black ties and ball gowns. I wanted to thank you."

He sucked in a cold breath. "For what exactly?"

"I want to have"—she tightened her grip—"a Pajama Rama. Isn't that simply brilliant?"

"A Pajama Rama?" he repeated. He had no idea what that was, but given his livelihood and her double clutch on his arm, Jillian was probably about to involve him.

"As I'm sure you know, the Elfcapades are Brooks Bend's twelve days of Christmas kindness. Evan and I selected a local children's hospital to be the beneficiary of the event. Money raised is going toward family services that typical health insurance doesn't cover."

"That's terrific." He'd admit it. Last night he had no interest in the Elfcapades his mother had referred to on the phone, but the more he learned about it, the town was really doing something special. He was enjoying his small contribution to tonight, even if it was only a couple of decorated cookies. Maybe he could also make a cash donation.

*Good idea.* He could talk to Charlie about it at the final stop—that was, if Jillian ever let go of his arm.

"We'd love to have you join us as our VIP."

"VIP?"

"You know. Meet the kids, take pictures. Maybe we could raffle off some of your pajamas?"

"Oh . . . um, well . . . I've got to get home to Manhattan." That was true. He could come back on Christmas to spend it with his family like he promised his sister, but he needed to be in his office at his drawing table with his sketch pad, creating mock-ups the rest of the time. Brooks Bend just didn't do anything for him. "I could donate a few pairs."

"Oh, goody, thanks." Jillian squeezed his arm even tighter. "Spencer Carmichael, you're the absolute best."

"You're welcome." Anything to have her let go and get the blood circulating in his arm. "I'll stop by your flower shop tomorrow."

They reached the mayor's three-story brick house, climbing up the cobblestone path to the front door. A lanky man in a preppy, pine-green sweater and red-collared shirt greeted people at the entrance.

Jillian gave the guy a hug. "Evan, I want you to meet Spencer Carmichael. Spencer, this is Mayor Hertzberg."

"Hello, Mayor, it's nice to meet you." Spencer extended a hand.

"It's nice to meet you, too, Spencer. Thank you for coming."

Jillian beamed at the two men. "Well, look at this. Two local celebrities in the flesh. Let me get a picture for the town's website. Hey, Lori." She pulled her phone out of her purse, waving over a pretty woman with short, black hair.

"Could you do me a favor and snap a picture of Evan and me with Spencer?"

Jillian stepped in between the men, putting her arms around both of them, her heavy perfume irritating his nose. "Evan's claim to fame is he was on *Jeopardy!*" she said through her wide smile.

"You don't say?" Spencer tilted his head down ever so slightly. Years of press had taught him the perfect chin angle for photos that could possibly trend on social media. "That's cool, man."

"Yeah, lost in the final round," Evan remarked. "Records trace the history of this sport to more than two thousand years ago, having started in China, Greece and Rome, but England can take credit for the game Americans know today." He shoved his hands in his pants pockets. "I thought it was tennis."

"What is soccer?" Spencer knew he was one hundred percent correct.

"Well, yes. That was it." Evan smirked, looking a bit put off.

Spencer lifted his knee, pretending to bounce a ball. "It was my game in high school. Ask me world geography or German scientists, I've got nothing."

"Is that right?" Evan pointed to the door, apparently finished with their conversation. "Good to finally meet you, Spencer. Enjoy your visit."

"I will." He left the couple and stepped into the three-story mansion, elegantly decorated with simple blue and silver wreaths. Dropping his jacket off at the coat check, he made his way into an enormous main room with exquisite dark-wood walls and a beautiful mahogany staircase.

A woman in a black waitstaff uniform approached with a tray. "Would you like a piece of peppermint bark?"

He'd really had his fill of cookies for one night, but didn't want to be rude. "Sure." He took a napkin and a piece of the pink bark, his gaze moving across the room, landing squarely on Charlie standing alone near the staircase. "If you don't mind, I think I'll take two, thank you."

He made his way to the mechanic, his pulse quickening as he approached. Yeah, he'd meant what he'd said to his sister earlier—he was quite content with being single. Still, partaking in pleasant conversation with a pretty woman who easily made him smile wasn't a bad way to top off the evening. "Hey. Can I offer you one last cookie?" he asked, holding out the peppermint bark.

"Well, technically, it's not a cookie, but thank you." She took it and bit down. "But, of course, it's amazing," she said, rolling her eyes.

"Didn't vote for Mayor Hertzberg in the last election?"

"No. I did." She laughed. "There wasn't a choice since he ran unopposed. He's my ex."

"Oh." How long ago did they break up? It was really none of his business. Plus, it wasn't like he was going to take his sister's advice and ask Charlie on a date.

A flash of him strolling down a snow-covered Main Street, linked arm in arm with Charlie, raced through his mind. He gulped and shoved his hands in his pockets. "The mayor seems like a nice guy."

"Yeah, we're still friends." She nodded to the entrance. "He's better suited for Jillian Fairweather."

He smiled. "So, it's the florist you're not a fan of."

"More like indifferent. She's good at keeping alive old high school pettiness that should be filed under ancient history." Charlie held up the bark. "Plus, she was bragging this morning at Dee Dee's about her grandma's infamous peppermint bark. I was truly hoping it would be mediocre." She took another bite. "I guess that's not in the spirit of Christmas, is it?"

He laughed and leaned in. "I won't tell. So, what you got there?" He pointed down to the notecard she was holding in her other hand.

"Just some remarks." She flashed a check behind her card. "As the sponsor of the event, I have to say a short thank-you and present the check." She sighed. "But I don't know why Evan's making such a big deal over it."

He followed her gaze to the mic and podium set up on the middle landing of the long staircase. "Well, everyone is certain to see you."

"Terrific," she said, and it wasn't a "can't wait to open the Christmas present that I've wanted all year" kind of terrific.

He studied her noticeable frown and the long crinkle line across her forehead. Was the color draining from her face? "Is everything okay? Can I grab you a drink? Maybe some water instead of cocoa?"

"I'm good. Thank you." She waved off his gesture. "I'm not much of a public speaker. I've never been good at it."

"Oh." She had a case of the nerves, and, no doubt, her zeroing in on the area where she'd be standing with all eyes on her wasn't helping. Maybe he could offer some advice. "I understand."

"You do?" Her question held considerable skepticism.

"Yeah, I've never liked talking to the press. Hate presenting to investors in stuffy board rooms. Doing live television interviews is the worst. Blech."

She lifted her lips slightly. "It probably sounds really silly to have stage fright. I mean, everyone here I've known pretty much since I was a child. It's not like it's a hostile crowd."

"You know what I do when I'm really nervous?"

She raised an eyebrow. "You're not going to tell me to imagine everyone in the room in their birthday suits. My dad's here somewhere, so I'd rather not."

He chuckled. Her humor was something he could work with. "Nah. It's too cold for that, but it is along those lines. I pretend my audience are all wearing hideous pajamas, and I'm about to save the day and put them in more sophisticated sleepwear couture."

"Seriously?"

"Yep. Super silly, and the cheesier the better. Sometimes I have a theme. Like before stepping onto the *Today Show* set, I envisioned all the hosts in a 'mythical creatures' line. All the anchors rocked the pink unicorn pajamas I imagined them in, complete with a tall horn." He waggled his eyebrows. "Want to try?"

"Unicorn pajamas," she deadpanned, and stared down at her card. "I should have stopped by the bar."

He placed his hands on her shoulders to turn her away from the staircase. Tiny jolts flew up his arms, and he immediately lifted his hands, rubbing his thumb over his tingling fingers.

*Stop it, man. She's terrified. Flirting with her isn't going to help.* He pointed to the crowd. "So tonight, we'll go with a Christmas theme. Everyone in this house is dressed as elves."

"Elves?"

"Yep, every single one of them." He pointed toward the mayor, who'd just entered the main room. "See your ex over there, Mr. *Jeopardy!*? He's the elves' ringleader with a gigantic, pointy green hat and enormous ears, and he's wearing green tights and really tacky red shoes that curl at the toes."

"Curl at the toes?" She gave him a short smile.

"Oh, yeah. Real winner, that one." He couldn't resist that last dig, even though he didn't really know the guy.

She started laughing. "I totally see it. 'Evan the Elf' has a nice ring."

Just then, Mayor Hertzberg approached with a leather

brown book, oblivious to their inside joke. "You ready, Charlie?" he asked, glancing down at his watch.

*What guy under forty wore one?* Okay, maybe the Apple Watch was popular. Spencer looked away, pretending to take in the nearby menorah display.

"Yeah," Charlie said, starting to climb the steps.

Spencer reached out and touched her arm, waggling his eyebrows. "Remember, they're all wearing elf costumes."

"Right," she said. "Full room of Santa's elves in here in red curly shoes. Got it."

Charlie followed the mayor up the stairs to the middle landing, standing by his side, her notecard in one hand and the paper check in the other.

The mayor tapped on the microphone. "Good evening, everyone. I'm delighted to welcome you to my home for the final stop on the Cookies and Cocoa Crawl on this fifth day of Elfcapades." He held up the book in his hand. "I'd like to start out by reading a poem that my great-great-grandmother wrote during her first Christmas in Brooks Bend."

Spencer shoved his hands in his pockets and listened politely, willing Charlie to look his way so he could give her an encouraging nod. When she finally did, she looked terror stricken.

Maybe he should stand toward the back, so as to not make her even more nervous. But instead, he made his way to the bar, mouthing a hello to Dee Dee Edwards, who was standing off to the side next to a man who looked to be her age.

"Poem, my eye. It's more like a short novel. He finds a way to read it every year," the old man said to Spencer. "I bet Dee Dee her White Christmas chili recipe that he'd do it tonight."

Spencer glanced over. He was pretty sure they hadn't met, but the guy's deep voice sounded really familiar. "I probably should have gotten some cocoa for this," he joked.

"You'll need something stronger. We're going to be here for a while," the man quipped back. "Spencer, I've been meaning to say hi all night. I'm Fred Dobbs."

"Oh, you're Charlie's dad." No wonder his voice sounded familiar. He'd talked to him on the phone twice today. "It's nice to meet you. How's my Audi coming along?"

"Good," was all he offered, but then added, "The part we need might take a few extra days to arrive. Definitely by next weekend."

"Next weekend," Spencer repeated. Well, that wouldn't work. "It's really going to take that long?"

"It could, but you know, Brooks Bend is a great place to spend the holidays," Fred offered.

"Especially when it snows," Dee Dee piped up.

"I'll remember that," he said politely. He was going to have to go with plan B and ask his sister to drive him back to the city.

"Charlie looks really nervous, Fred," Dee Dee commented.

Fred adjusted his glasses. "I shouldn't have made her go up there without me. I was hoping it would help boost her self-confidence. There are so many big changes in her future. I wanted her to see that she's in the driver's seat in facing her fears head-on and conquering them before she leaves. Maybe I should go pump the brakes."

Spencer stood quietly, listening to Fred's driving metaphors. What big changes were in Charlie's future? Was she leaving Brooks Bend, and where was she going? Those questions intrigued him for some reason.

His gaze zoomed across the room and up the stairs; the words of the mayor faded into white noise as he took in Charlie, her long, wavy blond hair falling well past her shoulders.

He might never see her again after tonight if she was leaving Brooks Bend.

He snapped his head back. A silly notion. He was leaving too. By Monday he'd be home in his Manhattan apartment, surfing Netflix, and shoving Chinese takeout into his mouth.

He stared down at the floor. That typical evening spent alone with *moo goo gai pan* suddenly seemed sad. Pathetic, really.

"And now it's my pleasure to introduce the sponsor of tonight's event, Charlie Dobbs from Dobbs Auto Repair and Body Shop."

Spencer lifted his head. Finally, Mayor Drip was done.

"Good evening, everyone," she blurted out before the

mayor had a chance to hand her the microphone. "Sorry, um . . . hi." She brought the mic up to her lips. "Yeah. Let me start over. Good evening, elves."

Polite, albeit confused, laughter came from the crowd.

Uneasiness crept up the back of his neck. *Oh no.* For the record, he didn't exactly tell her to call everyone elves. That was supposed to be between him and her.

"It's really my proud honor . . . um . . .uh." She stumbled over her words. "Uh . . . our proud honor to host the fifth day of Elfcapades. Uh, Evan—I mean, Mayor Hertzberg—is the host here . . . with, um . . . Jillian . . . his girlfriend. I'm just the sponsor."

She shut her mouth and closed her eyes. It was obvious that she was at a loss for words and had completely abandoned the speech on the index card she was now holding down to her side.

Her evident humiliation rushed through him, and his throat thickened. His advice had only made things worse.

*I can't let this continue.*

"If you'll both excuse me," he said to Fred and Dee Dee. His experience in public speaking, thinking on the fly, and rolling with the punches were all about to come in handy. He moved through the crowd to the front. He wasn't quite sure what he was doing, but he wasn't going to let Charlie embarrass herself any longer.

He stepped up to the stairs, his sister touching his arm. "Spencer, what are you doing?"

All of a sudden, the perfect idea came to him. "Changing up my process," he repeated her advice, giving a wink.

Charlie needed an excuse to explain her stammering and help save face, and he was about to hand her a big one. He reached the middle landing and gave her an encouraging smile, pointing at the microphone in her hand. "May I?"

Her face froze, but she moved to the side, away from the podium.

"Thank you." He stepped behind the podium. "Hi, everyone. For those of you I haven't met, I'm Spencer Carmichael. A proud Brooks Bend resident." He raised a fist high. "Go Beagles."

There were a few acknowledging hoots and dog barks coming from the crowd.

"It's so good to be back in my hometown to celebrate with all of you the fifth day of Elfcapades, but I have to apologize," he said, ready to drop some suspense. The room suddenly quieted on cue. "You see, right before she came up here, I sprang something big on Charlie. We're talking huge, and I shouldn't have done that." He glanced over just in time to see her head cock to the side. "It left her a little tongue-tied. Totally my fault."

He turned back to the crowd. "You see, as many of you know, my livelihood is designing Christmas pajamas. I'm currently working on next year's design and have been asked to immerse myself in the holidays to come up with a new, must-have creation. After today, I realized that there's no place better to be in than Brooks Bend to really feel the holiday spirit. Am I right?"

The crowd responded with resounding claps and cheers.

"But I'll admit, when it comes to small-town holiday charm, well, I'm a bit rusty. I need someone to help me design something that embodies an iconic Brooks Bend Christmas. Someone who fully embraces all of the wonderful traditions this town offers year after year."

He turned back to Charlie, taking in her lowered lashes. She was either going to be fully on board with what he was about to say or think he'd lost his mind.

And maybe he had, but knowing that Charlie might be leaving Brooks Bend made him suddenly want to stay. He took a deep breath. "I've asked Charlie Dobbs to design next year's Spencer Carmichael exclusive pajamas."

She opened her mouth to speak but shut it as loud applause erupted with a "Way to go, Charlie," from her father in the back.

"So, here's the plan. Charlie's going to get to work designing, and we're going to unveil her fantastic creation on the twelfth day of Elfcapades," he continued. Once he was done with this off-the-cuff presentation, he had a lot of explaining to do. At the moment, Charlie looked gobsmacked.

"And there's more. While Charlie's designing a new S.C. original, I'm very excited to participate in the event in a special way. Jillian, would you like to come up and say a few words about the Pajama Rama?"

Jillian emerged from the crowd. "Yes, of course. I'd be happy to." She climbed the steps and took the microphone.

"Charlie, I can explain." He turned to see a grimacing mayor standing alone.

SPENCER RACED DOWN the stairs, pretty sure he'd made it to the top of the auto mechanic's naughty list for that stunt.

Yeah, his idea was half-baked, but he wasn't ready to toss it out just yet. He raced through the house. Picking up his jacket at coat check, he hurried out the door and down the long driveway. Charlie was headed in the direction of his parents', no doubt to retrieve her truck.

"Charlie, wait up," he said, finally catching up to her.

"Spencer. It's been a long night, and it's nowhere near over for me. I have so much to do." She jostled the three boxes and clipboard she was carrying in her arms. "Go back and enjoy the party. They're probably about to announce the best cocoa winner."

"I think I'm crawled out. Besides, I'm sure my dad has it in the bag." He fell into step with her and caught his breath. "I'll lend a hand. What do you need me to do?"

She picked up her pace. "I'm good. You've done enough for tonight."

Okay, he deserved her coldness. "Look, I'm really sorry

about what happened. I was just trying to help."

"Help?" That got a sarcastic laugh. She appeared to be on a mission to ditch him.

The last thing he was going to say was that she was choking back there. "You seemed to be at a loss for words. I wanted to offer a reason for why you were a little . . . tongue-tied."

"So you decided to tell the whole town that their car mechanic is now making your iconic jammies by next Saturday?" she asked, shaking her head.

*Pajamas.* He shoved his hands in his jacket pockets. This wasn't the time to correct her. "I know it sounds completely bonkers. It's an idea that just sorta came to me."

"It just came to you that a woman you barely know who changes car oil for a living should make your jammies?"

Okay, they were going to have to work on what she called them, but, yes, that's exactly what happened. For some reason, this woman was inspiring him.

Maybe a few days spent with Charlie was all that was needed to jumpstart his creativity.

Now he had to get her to agree to his idea. "I know it seems crazy, but hear me out. I was hanging with your father at the bar, and I just kind of went with the moment." He paused, adding, "The idea was impromptu, but I still think it's a good one."

She stopped in her tracks. "What did my dad say to you?"

"Nothing." It didn't seem appropriate to bring up her lack of self-confidence or her dad's wanting to prepare her for big things coming up in her future, whatever they were. "I just realized that"—he waved his hand in the air—"you know . . . Christmas."

"And so do you," her voice rose. "Everyone does. It happens on December twenty-fifth every year. Every. Single. Year."

"Yeah, but you really get into the spirit of it. Look at the thought you put into tonight's event."

"I was just the sponsor." She readjusted her grip around the boxes. "It was my job."

"No. No." He shook his head. "You're selling yourself short, and not only tonight's event. What about the way you rattled off all those traditions you do every year? You make the Pizza & Pop Shop's Christmas pizza sound magical."

She gave him serious side-eye. Shoot. She wasn't buying it. "Spencer, everyone has Christmas traditions."

"Not everyone." His head dropped down to his jacket zipper. He certainly didn't. He lifted his chin. "Besides, you're the one who suggested you should make my pajamas. I thought about it, and I think it's a great idea."

"So much so that you decided to announce it to all my friends and family without even asking me?" she asked, her voice fired up.

Okay, she had a point. That had been wrong of him.

"I'm sorry how that went down." But he wasn't sorry

about what he did, and he'd dissect the reasons behind it another time. Right now, he needed to get her to agree.

They reached his parents' house and made their way to her truck. "I know it sounds zany." He held out his hands to hold her boxes so she could fish her keys out of her purse. "But Charlie, I've been struggling. You have such fond memories of Christmas here in Brooks Bend, and you still do many of those things each year." He nodded down to the box of cards. "Plus, I know you're creative."

She yanked her truck door open. "With paper and a glue gun! I don't know the first thing about fashion design."

He shook his head. "You don't have to. All I need is you to create a prototype. Something I could then turn into a professional design." He handed her one box at a time. "I'd give you full concept credit."

"Spencer, even if I wanted to help, and I'm definitely not saying I will"—she took her clipboard back and held it up to his face—"look at this long list. I don't have a lot of free time on my hands these days."

"May I?" His gaze moved down the long list. "What if I do these things for you? Would that free up your time?"

That offer got a raised eyebrow. "You want to do the things on my list?"

"Sure. Why not?" He zeroed in on the first few. "I can cut down a Christmas tree, no problem, and how hard could it be to replace transmission fluid? The transmission is under the hood, right?"

That got her to laugh, barely registrable, but it was definitely a sound of amusement. She folded her arms. "You really want me to help you, the legendary Spencer Carmichael, design pajamas?"

Call him crazy, but he'd never been surer of an impulsive decision. "Yes, and I don't know how legendary I am. Tell you what. Let's meet tomorrow morning at Dee Dee's Diner for breakfast. We'll go over assignments and officially make the handoff."

She bit down on her lip. "I guess I could. That is, meet you for breakfast. I love Dee Dee's eggnog waffles, and they won't be on the menu after the holidays."

"See! Another Christmas tradition. You're a natural at this, Charlie Dobbs."

"Uh-huh." She narrowed her lashes and took the clipboard back, tossing it into the passenger seat. "I'll see you tomorrow at eight."

Maybe it was her taste buds that ultimately won her over, but he'd take it. "Perfect. Don't forget to bring your to-do list. And, hey, if you have a picture of your tree from last year, can you bring that too?"

"I'll see you in the morning, Spencer," was all she said before she hopped into her truck.

"I'm looking forward to it. And don't do anything on that list. Leave it *all* to me." He closed her driver's-side door, then watched her start the tow truck and back out onto the street.

In an alternate universe, at this precise moment, he'd be sipping a cocktail while enjoying a warm ocean breeze from his hotel balcony.

He sucked in his cold cheeks while listening to the sound of Charlie's truck tires running over the crunchy snow.

This sound was way better.

# Chapter Seven

CHARLIE DRAINED HER second cup of Dee Dee's coffee and arched her back, her gaze moving over the different design ideas she'd spent the last twenty minutes scribbling onto her notepad.

Gingerbread men bobbing in hot chocolate. Snowmen sledding down ski slopes. Tiny reindeer flying in a star-filled sky over Brooks Bend . . .

"Oh, this is a waste of my time." She flipped her notepad to the first page. "I fix cars for people who need to get back on the road, not fledgling careers of famous sleepwear designers so everyone can look cute on Christmas morning."

She reached for her Sharpie and scribbled at the very top of her checklist, "Talk to Spencer." He'd just have to come up with a new plan to save his reputation that didn't involve her.

There was way too much that she needed to get done, including getting ready for her job interview on Monday.

Her thoughts drifted back to last night. Despite her "perfect ten" swan dive into the deep end of humiliation in front of the entire town, the crawl had started out, honestly, terrific. She'd collected so many signed cards to go with the donated cookies.

She glanced up at the photo of Spencer, her pulse quickening. Yeah, their time alone in the Carmichael kitchen decorating Christmas cookies had been fun too.

If only she'd found a way to skip the last stop. If she hadn't made such a fool of herself at Evan's, Spencer would have never made that ridiculous announcement.

She wasn't naïve. He pretty much admitted last night what he'd done was thrown her a lifejacket to save her from drowning. "He should have let me sink," she mumbled.

People would have forgotten the crummy speech.

But they'd never forget this. It wouldn't be long before the entire town knew about Spencer's big announcement at the mayor's house.

She flipped the notepad back to her bad ideas. The last thing she needed was another round of humiliation, but that would surely happen if she went through with Spencer's ridiculous plan and failed.

She took a long sip of her coffee. Putting an end to this was imperative before it even got started. Perhaps she wasn't alone in that thinking. Maybe a good night's sleep was all Spencer had needed to come to his senses. There was no way she was qualified to design a set of Christmas jammies, and certainly not his iconic ones.

Never mind a bad business decision . . . it was a waste of everyone's time.

"Another cup, dear?"

She looked up to see Dee Dee holding a full pot of coffee. "I'd love one. Thank you."

"Are you working on your design for Spencer?" she asked, pointing to the notepad.

"Um, yes . . . I mean, no." She leaned back. "I'm just waiting for him to arrive so I can tell him I'm out. It's silly to think that I can help him."

Dee Dee opened her mouth and then shut it, letting a couple of seconds go by before asking, "Why can't you?"

Did she really need to state the obvious to her friend? "I should be inserting an oil dipstick into a car engine right now." She raised her Sharpie in the air. "Not jotting down terrible sleepwear design concepts that even a mannequin wouldn't wear. I'm a mechanic. That's what I do."

"But you won't be one for much longer," Dee Dee countered, placing her free hand on her hip.

Charlie pressed her lips together. *Of course Dee Dee knows about my job interview.* She'd filled her dad in on the conversation with David yesterday at the shop. He'd been ecstatic, bringing her in for a giant bear hug.

Though she'd told him it was just one interview and to not get too excited, he'd evidently blabbed the news to Dee Dee at some point during the crawl. "Yeah, but I'm considering going into interior product development for automobiles, not creating pajamas for an established designer."

"Well, I think this could be a nice bridge for you."

"Bridge?" What did Dee Dee mean by that?

"My mother gave me some great advice once when I was stuck in a miserable office job. She told me, 'Dee Dee, keep your big brown eyes wide open because life always drops in a big sign when it's time to take a pause and do something different.' And you know what?"

"What?"

"One night I was walking past the diner after a particularly miserable day at work, and ole Mack Lawson was hanging a Help Wanted sign in the window for a short-order cook. I'd always loved cooking, even as a child. My mom's advice rang through my head at that precise moment. I knew it was my sign."

She continued, "I went straight in and yanked down that sign, telling Mack he had a new short-order cook. I worked part time for a year before quitting my office job to work in the diner full time." She straightened her apron. "And the rest is history. Working here nights and weekends all those years ago boosted my confidence, propelling me over the bridge. When Mack retired, I was in prime position to take over."

Charlie cocked her head. While she appreciated Dee Dee's pep talk, how could designing for Spencer factor into what she'd ultimately be doing when her father sold the auto shop? "You think Spencer crashing his luxury car into a snowbank is a big sign for me to do something different with my life?"

Dee Dee shrugged and straightened the coffee cup and silverware opposite Charlie. "Maybe this is your chance to test the waters. Do something that doesn't involve engine grease. Take a few steps onto that bridge. Enjoy the journey. Go with the flow, like I did all those years ago. You just might like what's waiting for you on the other side."

"Hmm . . . go with the flow." Charlie reached for the little cow creamer and poured some into her coffee, then gave it a stir. Dee Dee could certainly throw out her metaphors to emphasize her point. "I don't know. I've got a lot to do to get ready for my interview and . . ." She paused, glancing up at the photo of Spencer. "I'm just not sure I can help him. Surely, there has to be a designer in Manhattan he can call on to assist him if he's really that blocked creatively. He probably has an assistant or someone junior under him."

"Tell you a little secret about our hometown hero that I doubt anyone, except maybe for Olivia and Earl, knows."

Charlie took her gaze off the photo and back to Dee Dee. "That he has an affinity for stuffed animals?"

Dee Dee chuckled. "Well, he might have an old Tickle Me Elmo, but no. I've known that kid his whole life and personally witnessed him spend hours upon hours right here in this very booth with his sketch pad and pencils, staring off into space. I'd bring him plates of my tater tots, and you know what he'd say?"

"That they're the best grated potatoes he'd ever eaten?"

With Dee Dee's homemade spicy mayo sauce, that statement was certainly true.

"Well, that too. No, he'd apologize for staying so long. He was just waiting for inspiration to strike to finish his art assignment, and he couldn't leave until it did. One night, he asked if he could hang out in the kitchen and draw me cooking during the dinner rush, so we set him up on a stool off to the side." She pointed to a framed picture of the diner's kitchen above the cash register. "He drew that beauty."

"Spencer drew that?" Charlie had always admired the pencil sketch of a younger Dee Dee cooking up a storm that captured perfectly the love she put into each and every meal.

"Uh-huh. He said watching me cook was all the inspiration he needed." She laughed. "So yes, it *was* my tater tots that inspired him—or at least got him an 'A' for that assignment."

Charlie settled back in the booth. "It's really sweet that you supported his early talent, but what does that have to do with me?"

"If he asked for your help, he must have been inspired by you."

"Me?" she asked, flattening a palm to her chest. "A small-town auto mechanic inspired the Man with the Bag?"

Dee Dee patted Charlie's shoulder. "My dear, you have so many untapped talents. You don't have to cross the bridge entirely, just start your journey. If it doesn't work out, I'm sure Spencer will be fine." Dee Dee nodded to the entrance as the man himself stepped through the glass door.

"Right." Charlie set aside her uncertainty, straightening her shoulders.

"Well, look who we have here." Spencer approached the table. "How did a guy get so lucky to see my favorite lady and my new apprentice in one spot?"

Charlie's heart began to accelerate as he kissed Dee Dee's cheek. In his hand was one of the red satin bags she remembered from the night of his accident.

She tugged up her overalls strap. Did Spencer have to look so cute in his parka and jeans? Maybe she should have waited to put on her work clothes until she got to the auto shop.

That thought deserved the mental slap she gave herself. She didn't need to dress up to impress this man today or any day. "Hi," she said.

"Hey." He took off his jacket and slid into the booth. "I'm glad you came."

She raised an eyebrow. "Did I have a choice?"

"You always have a choice, Charlie."

He shot her a wide smile that somehow had the magical power of turning up her temperature. She scratched her throat. "Dee Dee, would I be able to get some water, please?"

"Of course." Dee Dee turned over the coffee cup and filled it for Spencer. "I'll get you both menus."

"No need for me, Dee Dee." He winked at Charlie. "I

hear the eggnog waffles are amazing. I'll take a stack."

"Make that two." Charlie held up her two fingers.

"Coming right up." Dee Dee grinned and mouthed, "Go with the flow" to Charlie. With a bounce to her hips, she disappeared behind the counter and through the kitchen.

"Um, about last night," Charlie began, folding her hands in her lap. There was no use waiting until their waffles arrived to have this conversation. "While I appreciate your help—"

"I see you brought your to-do list," he cut her off, nodding to the clipboard. "So, lay it on me." He reached for a sugar packet and ripped it open, then poured the contents into his coffee and stirred. "What tasks do you need done today?"

"You didn't change your mind?" This was insane. How could he have not come to the same conclusion she had?

"No." He shook his head. "Did you?"

*Yes!* She blinked over at him for a second, the warmth in his bright blue eyes causing her chest to tighten. Why did this man want her help?

Dee Dee's advice ran through her head. Yes, it was true. Everything was going to change in the new year. Maybe she should consider taking that first step now if this was a bridge to the new life where a confident, self-assured Charlie could do whatever she set out to do. Something entirely different than rotating tires.

But was it making Christmas jammies?

She broke their eye contact, scanning her clipboard. She couldn't deny that it would be nice to have some help with her list. With another pair of hands, she could focus on the really important things she needed to get done, which included buying a suit for her interview, since she didn't own one.

Maybe she could amuse him for one day and give him two or three things to do while she was Christmas ideating. "Well." She set down her cup. "I had planned on running over to Greenville. A performance part I need to install in Mrs. Lathrop's old Chevy will be ready for pickup at the car's dealership."

His eyebrows furrowed. "Lillian Lathrop on Robbins Road? She's still in Brooks Bend?"

"You know her?"

"Yeah, she was friends with my mother and gave me piano lessons one summer. I had a massive crush on her daughter, Brenda. She went off to Boston University my junior year." He grinned and lifted his coffee cup to his lips. "It broke my heart."

Charlie smirked. High school Spencer was no doubt just as cute as the thirty-something one sitting across from her currently sipping his coffee.

"Well, Brenda's now happily married in Bangor, about to have a baby any day, and Lillian's eager to get there for the birth of her first granddaughter. She wants to leave tomorrow morning before the weather gets bad. They're expecting a major snowstorm to come from the north. Once I have the part, it shouldn't take me too long to install it this afternoon."

"Easy enough. My sister loaned me her minivan. I can zip on over. What else do you need done?"

Charlie stared down at her list, a mix of work and personal to-dos. He certainly couldn't try on interview suits for her. She reached for the Sharpie and blackened out that item.

Maybe stick to things that could inspire his inner Christmas. Perhaps he'd come up with a new, fantastic design on his own and this nonsense would end. "I was going to cut down my Christmas tree."

"I remember. Did you bring a picture of the one you got last year?"

She stared at him for a beat. What an odd request that was no doubt part of the Spencer Carmichael creative process. "I've got one on my phone." She gave in and reached for her phone to text it.

"What's your number?" On no planet did she ever imagine having Spencer's phone number, let alone texting him a photo of her Christmas tree with its popcorn string garland and homemade wooden ornaments.

A second later, Spencer's cell phone chimed, and he held it up. "Hmm, the lighting is a bit dark, and I can't see the ceiling. I guess it'll have to do," he said, sounding disappointed as he shoved his phone in his jacket pocket. "What else?"

"Just some errands around town. Oh, we're also planning to hang some Christmas lights on the outside of the garage." He certainly was tall enough for that assignment. "You could help my dad if you'd like."

He grimaced. "I'd like to pass on that last one."

Was he seriously triggered by Christmas lights? She studied him for a second. "They're not going to catch fire."

"I'd still like to pass."

"Okay, well . . ." She eyed the list. "We're also painting the inside of the shop before potential buyers come in to see the place. I picked out the color yesterday afternoon."

"You're selling the body shop?"

"My dad is," she corrected him. "He's retiring in the new year."

"And you're not taking over?" he asked as Dee Dee set down two plates stacked with three fluffy eggnog waffles drizzled in maple syrup.

"No," she replied ever so quickly, attacking her waffles. Spencer had just poked a sore spot. It wasn't that she wanted to take over running an auto shop on her own, but that her dad hadn't even considered that as an option had been a blow to her pride. "I'm exploring other options at the moment," she said in between bites.

"Well, that's great. Change is good."

"So I've heard." She lowered her lashes, glancing in Dee Dee's direction. The diner owner gave her a thumbs-up sign.

"How are your waffles?" she asked, changing the subject. Spencer didn't need to know that her life was in one big state of flux.

He took a bite, and his eyes rolled way back. "Oh wow. Man, if these were on the menu when I was a kid, I may have never left."

"They are one of a kind." She smiled over at him. What would it have been like if Spencer had never left Brooks Bend or commuted into the city? Would they have been friends?

"Oh, I have something for you." He picked up the red satin bag and set it on the table.

"You're giving me a set of flammable pajamas?"

"Very funny. No." He shook his head. "Just some tools that I thought might be helpful. I'm guessing, given your livelihood, you understand how important the right tool is to getting the job done."

"Tools. Getting the job done," she repeated, setting down her fork and rubbing her hands together. "*Now* you're finally speaking my language," she joked, opening the pipe cleaner drawstring and pulling out an iPad, a silver rectangular container, and a red rubber ball.

She flipped open the container to see thin sharp pencils and a couple of chubby sticks.

"You're holding my personal sketch kit," he boasted proudly. "You'll find standard black, white, and charcoal pencils along with typical Christmas colors. There's some smudge sticks in there as well."

Smudge sticks? How did one smudge? "Oh, I don't want to use up your pencils." She shut the kit and picked up her Sharpie, waving it in the air. "I'll just use this."

"Nonsense. These are designed for sketching. Trust me. You are going to want these."

"Okay." She set the pencil kit aside. Should she admit now that her drawing abilities were limited to stick people, snowflakes, and maybe a Christmas tree with a simple star on its top? She picked up the iPad and red rubber ball. "What are these for?"

"My files can be accessed on my iPad, including past designs and prototypes that were good but never made the cut. I thought maybe they'd help spark your design."

She gulped. *My design.* He said it like it was a given inevitability. "Thank you. And this?" she asked, holding up the rubber ball, bouncing it on the table and catching it in her palm.

"My secret weapon."

"A red rubber ball?" She held it at eye level. No wonder he needed her help.

"Yes. It's how I ideate. I usually carry it around in my pocket when I'm brainstorming. Mrs. McCoy gave it to me my senior year."

"The high school art teacher?"

"Yeah. You had her too?"

"Of course. Everyone did." She shrugged because she

wasn't going to overplay her art skills and pretend to be a van Gogh. "I took her in ninth grade, but after that . . . well, I was more of a shop elective kind of girl."

He grinned, setting his fork down on his cleaned plate. "I wonder if we ever bumped into each other in high school."

That idea sent skittles up her back. What a weird thing to wonder. "Maybe if you hung out in the library."

"Nah." He sprawled out his arms along the booth. "If I wasn't running down a soccer field, I was right here in this very booth."

"Yeah, I know," she quipped, nodding up to the picture of him.

"Don't knock the power of Dee Dee's home cooking and the ambiance of this diner. Some of my best work was done here."

"I'll remember that." Her gaze zoomed over to the intricate diner kitchen sketch. Despite this being a loony idea born out of his kindness to not let her fall on her face, if Dee Dee was right and somehow Charlie had inspired him, maybe she could help him get back on track. "We should probably get started."

"Right." He reached for his jacket. "I've got a tree to cut."

She gathered up Spencer's things and placed them in the satin bag. "And I have jammies to design."

"About that . . ."

Her hand froze inside the bag. Had he changed his mind?

"You know what? Not important." He pulled out his wallet to pay for breakfast.

She tugged on the bag's drawstrings. "Before we part ways, do you mind if we do the first thing on my list together?" It was a priority item for this morning that she really didn't want to miss.

"Together." He waggled his eyebrows. "What? You don't trust me with engine oil?"

She laughed, although she should probably cross out anything on the list that involved his getting under a car hood. "I was planning on dropping off last night's donated cookies and cards to Lakeview." She slid on her coat. "It's too early to go to Greenville for Lillian's part, and I think you should wait until the temperature goes up a bit before cutting down my tree. We can take my truck, and I'll bring you back here when we're done."

"Sure. I'd like to help, and I want to make a cash donation while we're there."

She glanced up at him. "You do?"

"Yeah."

"That's really nice of you," she said, trying not to sound so surprised. Perhaps Spencer was generous with his charitable giving this time of year. That is, before he hightailed it to the Bahamas.

"What can I say?" He set a twenty- and ten-dollar bill on

the table to take care of their breakfast and tip. "Maybe I've caught some of your Christmas spirit."

Her cheeks warmed, despite his making it sound like her holiday cheer was a deadly infectious disease. She looked away just in time to catch Dee Dee holding a coffeepot, making a wave motion with her free hand.

Charlie took a deep breath and clutched the satin bag, following Spencer out of the diner to her truck. *Okay, I'm going with the flow.*

A wave of nausea slammed through her. Would Dee Dee's advice only lead to more public humiliation if she couldn't deliver the perfect jammies idea?

# Chapter Eight

"SO, DO YOU drive anything else, Charlie?" Spencer asked, sliding into the truck.

"If you mean do I have another car, I have a Honda that once was my mother's, but this time of year, I prefer driving the truck." She turned on the ignition and pulled out of the parking spot. "It's great in the winter."

"I bet." He paused for a second to slip on his seat belt. "Hey, did your dad tell you that my car might not be ready until next weekend?"

"Yeah. He suggested last night that might be the case."

"What do you think?"

She fiddled with the heat. That was nice of him. She rarely felt inferior for being a woman mechanic or Fred Dobbs's daughter, but every once in a while, someone would dismiss her diagnosis and ask for her dad's second opinion. "It's possible. I can take another look this morning."

"That would be great. Thank you." He peered out the window as they made their way down Main Street and up the hill that would take them to the Lakeview. "Wow. It's funny how this place never changes. I learned how to drive on this back road. Mom was afraid to take me in"—he held his fingers up in air quotes—"Main Street traffic."

"Three cars on the same road *can* be stressful for new drivers. Ever miss small-town life?"

"Nah." He threaded his fingers and cracked his knuckles. "I'm more of a bustling city guy."

*Of course you are.* Charlie focused on the gravel road. A place like Brooks Bend, without a theater, fancy steak restaurants, and sports teams, would probably bore him to death. "Well, we'll get you back to that bustle as soon as we can."

"But not until you come up with a design. I'm committed to staying here through the twelfth day of Elfcapades." He relaxed back into the seat and stretched his legs out under the front dash.

"No pressure there." She turned the radio dial, landing on a Christmas station and adjusting the volume.

"So, tell me about you."

An electric charge raced through her fingertips, sending the Christmas music louder and louder. "Sorry," she shouted, turning the volume knob way down. "What do you want to know?"

"Did you always want to be an auto mechanic?"

"I wouldn't say always. I've grown up fixing cars all my life, working part time for my dad in high school and during college breaks."

"Wow. That's cool. Hey, I wonder if you ever worked on

my first Jeep. I took it in there a few times before I went off to college."

"Probably not." She couldn't recall ever seeing an eighteen-year-old Spencer and had a sneaking suspicion she'd remember those blue eyes. "I hung out in the shop sometimes after school and did my homework in my dad's back office while he worked, but I didn't get my hands greasy until my junior year."

"Gotcha. Where did you go to college?"

"UConn."

He chuckled. "A Husky."

She smiled. "After I graduated, I was having a tough time getting a job in my major. The economy was in the tank back then. So I started working for my dad full time, doing way more under the hood than he ever let me do in high school or college." She continued up the steep road, shifting the truck's gears. "I fell in love with it."

"Really? Car maintenance?"

"Yeah." He could straighten his cocked, judgmental head. Just because it wasn't a high- paying, white-collar career didn't mean she couldn't love her job just as much as he did his. "Every day, every vehicle has a different problem to solve. Just when I think my day is going to be dull, I get a call from Sheriff Thompson."

"Because some fool took The Vine in the snow to shave off time."

"Something like that." She gave him a playful grin. "I

love my job—car grease and all."

"But you're looking to do something different now?"

She took a deep breath. *Geez. Did everyone in this town know?* "Well, yes. I'm considering a career move."

"Your dad mentioned last night some big changes were in store for you."

"My dad has a family friend who owns an automotive design firm. They have a position open developing interior products."

"Is that something you'd like to do?"

"Maybe. I like to tinker every now and then. Are your socks clean?"

"Huh?"

"Are your socks clean?" she repeated the question. "If they are, try out the floor mat I made." She reached over, pulled up a cord, and plugged it into her charger outlet. "It's also a heated foot massager."

He slid off his shoe. Placing his foot on the mat, he leaned back and closed his eyes. "Oh, yeah."

"I made it for my mom. She used to like to ride around town with me." Her mom had wanted to spend as much time as she could with Charlie in those last few months before she became too ill to leave the house. Charlie had made sure her rides were especially warm and cozy.

"So . . ." She glanced over at Spencer, now rubbing both his feet over the massager. "Are you enjoying your time in Brooks Bend?"

"You know, I think I am. Last night was a lot of fun."

"Well, this really was the week for you to crash your car, in my opinion."

"Why's that?"

"Because there are seven more days of Elfcapades, and tonight, the sixth night, is not to be missed."

That got him to laugh. "It's at the ice rink, right? My niece informed me this morning that I would be taking her and my nephew. She's very excited about the Christmas goose up for grabs."

Charlie grinned. The Six-Geese-a-Laying Contest was by far one of her favorite Elfcapades events, but with Spencer's big reveal at Evan's last night occupying her waking thoughts, she'd forgotten all about it. "Well, I don't want to brag, but you're actually riding alongside the reigning champ."

"Of the Christmas goose?"

"Three years in a row." She held up three fingers. "It's proudly displayed in my apartment. I have no intentions of taking it out of my home tonight for very long."

Spencer cocked an eyebrow. "That sounds like a challenge. What must one do to upset your reign?"

She wasn't worried in the slightest. Someone might beat her tonight, but it wasn't going to be the man whose Christmas tradition until now had included a beach towel, sunscreen, and sand. "You'll see, but you should probably bundle up. The event is all outdoors and can go well into the night."

"Noted."

She slowed down as they reached the top of the hill. "So, do you have any tips for me for designing Christmas jammies?" If she was going to do this, she might as well pick his brain before they parted ways.

He slid on his shoes. "Tip number one. They're pajamas."

"What's the difference?"

He was silent for a beat. "I just prefer pajamas. It's part of my brand."

*Okay.* The brand she saw splattered all over the snow two nights ago. Maybe step one should be to call them jammies. She kept that suggestion to herself.

"Tip two," he continued. "You'll want to think of simple Christmas concepts. Universal symbols of the holidays are best sellers. I'd probably stay away from anything that's too difficult to grasp." He let out a deep sigh. "Like my French hens. Also, you'll want to be careful that it's not too cutesy. No Christmas bears or toy nutcrackers."

"Got it. No cutesy." Her gingerbread men floating in hot chocolate she'd scribbled down earlier probably wouldn't cut it.

They reached the nursing home, parked, and, headed in, each carrying the cookie containers and cards.

"Charlie!" Rosie Pritchett greeted them from behind the front desk. Charlie had personally winterized Rosie's car last week with a strong recommendation that she replace all four of her worn tires this spring. "We've been waiting for you all morning. The residents are so excited to taste this year's cookies."

Charlie grinned at the nurse, setting her containers on the front desk. "The wait is over. We've got all kinds to satisfy any sweet tooth. Sugar cookies, snickerdoodles, gingerbread men, and peppermint bark. And Nurse Rosie, this is Spencer Carmichael. He personally decorated *two* of the sugar cookies." She tossed him a wink with that little dig, just in time to catch the amusement in his eyes.

"It's so nice to finally meet you, Spencer. I'm a big fan." Rosie held out her hand. "I just loved the pajamas you designed last year. My cat, Sylvie, can't get enough of the feathers every time I wear them."

"Great," he deadpanned, but grinned nevertheless. "I could have made a mint marketing them as cat toys."

Charlie couldn't help placing an empathetic hand on his shoulder, and when she did—those electric jolts shot straight up her arm this time. She removed her hand and tucked it safely in her jacket pocket, rubbing her tingling finger pads along the jacket's lining. "Rosie, we also have signed holiday cards. Enough for all the residents to get one, maybe two."

Rosie beamed. "Thank you so much for this special treat and selecting the nursing home for one of the twelve days of Christmas kindness again this year." She pointed to an old woman inching her way down the hallway with a walker.

"Molly has been on cookie patrol since I started my shift." She called out to the woman, "Ms. Molly, come meet Charlie and Spencer."

The old woman maneuvered her walker toward them, her crinkled eyes fixated on Spencer as she said a loud hello.

"Charlie and Spencer, I'd like you to meet Molly Murdoch," Rosie made introductions, cranking up the volume on her voice. "Ms. Molly, this is Charlie Dobbs and Spencer Carmichael. Spencer makes Christmas pajamas."

"Would you like a cookie, Ms. Molly?" he asked, opening the lid to the top container.

"Oh, wow. Look at that." Molly peered in and selected one of Spencer's decorated snowflakes. "Why, this is the most beautiful snowflake I've ever seen. It looks like the real thing."

Charlie caught the "see?" look Spencer threw her way. She reached into the container and pulled out the top red envelope she'd flagged last night. "Molly, here's a card, too, from Spencer. Happy holidays."

The old woman's face lit up. "May I take another cookie to Orlena?" She reached in and grabbed the second snowflake Spencer had decorated.

"Orlena's her roommate," Rosie explained. "Although, they're not speaking at the moment. I doubt Orlena will ever see that cookie."

"Oh, Rosie." Spencer reached into his back pocket and pulled out his wallet. "I'd like to make a donation." He handed her two hundred-dollar bills. "If it's okay with you, I'd also like to make a call and have a couple boxes of last year's holiday pajamas sent over here in an assortment of different sizes. You could have them sometime next week."

"That's so generous of you. Our seniors will love them." Rosie clapped her hands and came around the counter, giving Spencer a warm hug and then doing the same to Charlie. "Thank you both so much. We are just so grateful for your generosity."

"We're happy to do it." Charlie smiled. "Everyone had so much fun making them." She laughed, adding, "And tasting them."

"If you both have time,"—Rosie motioned down the hall—"you could hand out the cookies in our cafeteria. I'm sure Molly's already made the big announcement that they've arrived. Nothing says Christmas like a little sugar with your oatmeal."

"Do we have time, boss lady?" Spencer asked, his sparkling blue eyes meeting Charlie's.

She blinked. *We.* Something about that question and the way he was looking at her caused her knees to shake. Plus, it was an upgrade from "tow lady."

"Sure. That'd be fun."

They followed Rosie down the hall, and in no time, were passing out cookies and chatting with the elderly folks seated at scattered tables around the room.

"Hi, would you each like to try a homemade Christmas

cookie?" Charlie approached a group of four old men seated around a table, instantly recognizing one as Mr. Dockstader, her father's accountant for many years before he retired. His red Toyota sedan was the first car she'd ever helped her dad rotate tires on when she was sixteen.

Mr. Dockstader's grin widened. "I know you. You're Fred Dobbs's daughter."

"That I am. Hi, Mr. Dockstader. It's so nice to see you."

He set his puzzle book to the side. "It's been years since I've been behind the wheel of a car." His bushy, salt-and-pepper eyebrows waggled. "Did your dad send you? Have you come to bust me out of this joint and take me for a spin in Fred's Mustang?"

Charlie chuckled. Her father had sold that jalopy years ago. "It's too cold for the top down. How about a cookie instead?" She pulled back the top to show off the selection inside.

"Thank you." Mr. Dockstader took the cookie and slid up his bifocals, staring up at Charlie. "Why, didn't you turn out to be a cutie?"

"Now don't be flirting with me, Mr. Dockstader. I don't want to get in trouble with any of your girlfriends in here."

"I won't tell if you don't." He laughed, pointing in Spencer's direction. "Is that your fella?"

"Oh, no. We're just . . ." She cocked her head in Spencer's direction. What were they, exactly? "He's kind of my . . . I guess I'd call him . . ." She focused on Mr. Dockstader. "His name is Spencer Carmichael, and he's visiting from Manhattan." There. No need to put a label on whatever Christmas pact they'd made.

"Well, I see he's quite popular with the ladies in here."

Charlie followed Mr. Dockstader's gaze, biting back a laugh at Molly and three additional silver-haired ladies vying for Spencer's attention. Molly had linked her arm through his.

She passed out cookies to the other seniors at the table before excusing herself. "Enjoy your treats and merry Christmas." She zigzagged through the tables to Spencer, who seemed thoroughly amused at all the elderly women fawning over him.

"You ready to get going?"

"Sure." He maneuvered his arm out of Molly's clutch and gave her shoulder a pat. "Ladies, it's been an absolute delight. I hope you enjoy the cookies, and I'll be sure to stop in with your pajamas before I leave town."

The women all waved as the two headed out of the cafeteria to the front exit. Charlie smirked, shaking her head. Someone seemed to be popular.

"What?"

"What what?" she asked, waving goodbye to Rosie and pulling out her knit hat she'd stuffed earlier in her jacket pocket.

"What's that look for?"

"Oh, nothing," she said, putting her hat on. "Do you

make new fans everywhere you go?"

He laughed. "What can I say? Women of a certain age dig me."

That really didn't surprise her. She pressed her lips together. But what did women his age think of him? Did he have a steady stream of girlfriends?

Her shoulders drooped. Was there someone special in his life?

She straightened and pushed open the glass door. Why did it matter? He was returning to New York City next weekend.

And she might be joining him soon. *Stop it.* It wasn't like they'd run into each other, and they definitely wouldn't be traveling in the same circles or living in the same neighborhood, for that matter. If she did get the job, she'd most likely have to find a tiny studio apartment she could afford, maybe in Brooklyn or Queens.

The thought of living anywhere but above the Pizza & Pop Shop made her chest tighten. She quietly made her way to the truck she'd probably also be giving up soon. Would she be able to acclimate to taking the train?

Did she even want to?

"Hey, everything alright?" he asked.

"Oh, yeah." His question brought her back to the moment. "Sorry, just thinking about . . ."

"Your to-do list," he finished her sentence.

"Yeah." She smiled, adding, "And what you did back

there. It was really nice of you to make a cash gift to the nursing home and offer to donate pajamas."

"Happy to do it." Spencer followed her out, zipping up his jacket. "Maybe I'll make that my new Christmas tradition."

"Well, it'd be a good one." She stopped behind her truck and nodded back toward the building. "I also believe you have two new superfans in Ms. Molly and Rosie."

"I knew my cookie design would be a huge hit." He slid into her truck's passenger side just as she jumped into the front seat. "One of a kind will always trump mass market."

"Yeah, and if you start now, maybe you'll have enough cookies for the entire nursing home for next Christmas," she joked, then started up the engine and proceeded down the hill.

Five minutes later, Charlie pulled up next to Kristina's minivan.

"Okay, time to get to work." He picked up her clipboard. "Want to meet up for some of Dee Dee's hot chocolate this afternoon and debrief?"

She opened her mouth, but paused for a beat. He was really committed to this . . . whatever *this* was.

A vision of them sitting in front of the Christmas tree in the square making their way through Dee Dee's generous whipped cream popped into head. "I think that'd be great. I should be done with Lillian's car by three o'clock."

"Okay then." He opened the passenger door. "Let's say

four o'clock."

"Sounds good." She reached out and tugged his jacket. "Only the first three items on the list need to be done today." They should be easy enough for him to accomplish. "The rest can wait."

"Great. Christmas tree, auto part, paint," he ticked off. "Got it. I'll head up to the Christmas tree lot soon."

"Thank you, and oh, one last thing. That part for Mrs. Lathrop will be in by noon, but the dealer is closing at one for their company holiday party, so best to get it right at noon. I've scheduled installation at two, so you have some time in between if you want to pick up the paint and then drop everything off at the shop."

"Will do." He stepped out of her truck, studying the list. "What do you have to talk to me about?"

"Talk to you about?"

He tapped the Sharpie to the top of her list where she'd scribbled *Talk to Spencer.* "It says here you need to talk to me."

"Yeah, I did want to talk to you, didn't I?" Dee Dee's advice ran through her head. *Go with the flow.*

She'd done that this morning and had a lot of fun with this man. If anything, maybe his help was a welcome distraction from her current anxieties about what her future held, and she'd still plow through her to-do list.

"Um . . ." She thought for a second. "My tree. I wanted to talk to you about selecting my Christmas tree. Please only get a four-foot one. Anything higher is, honestly, such a pain to carry up and down the stairs." She pointed to the Pizza & Pop Shop. "My apartment is above there. You can set the tree in the stairwell, and I can bring it up tonight."

"Roger that. This is going to be fun. Have a great day ideating, Charlie. Can't wait to hear all about your initial designs."

*Oh, right.* Her end of this deal. She'd have to be prepared to share something when they met up this afternoon. Maybe she could solicit Gwen's help while she was trying on business suits. "I'll get to work, but I can't promise I'll be a Vera Wang or Stella McCartney right out the gate."

"I'm betting that what Charlie Dobbs comes up with will be a festive, holiday, one-of-a-kind sensation."

*Well, that's one of us.*

"I'll meet you back here for that cocoa." He tucked her clipboard under his arm. "I've got to pop into Brooks Buds and speak to Jillian about donating a few pairs of adults' and kids' pajamas to the Pajama Rama, and then I'll go pick out your tree."

"Thank you. Don't forget Lillian's part at noon," she said, turning up her radio. He gave her a thumbs-up before shutting the passenger door.

Spencer headed down Main Street just as the Christmas song "The Man with the Bag" blared throughout the cabin. Her heart raced.

Two days ago, she'd never met Spencer Carmichael.

Now he was in her life for the holidays.

She clutched the steering wheel with both hands, resting her chin on it, and watched him disappear into Brooks Buds.

"Charlotte Elizabeth Dobbs, what on earth are you getting yourself into?"

# Chapter Nine

"I STILL CAN'T believe you're designing Christmas pajamas for the legendary Spencer Carmichael. Maybe he'll ask for your help every year," Gwen said from the other side of the dressing room stall. "You two will become the renowned dynamic duo of the sleepwear industry."

"Whoa. Slow your roll, please." Charlie slid on the reddish-purple suit jacket, barely recognizing herself in the mirror. "It's one design idea, and it's really not that big of a deal. Anyone can help him. If you've got a good one, I'm all ears."

"Let me think . . . I know! What about puppies and kittens wearing Christmas jammies? Growing up, my brother and I used to dress our terrier, Rosco, and orange tabby, Roxy, in them every year without fail." She giggled. "Rosco loved stretching out in his flannel jammies by the fireplace, but Roxy, not so much."

"I don't know. It's a fun idea, but it might be too adorable. Spencer told me specifically no cutesy designs." Charlie ran a hand down the hem of the matching purple skirt, glancing down at her bare, pasty-white legs and black wool socks. For her interview, she'd have to ditch the work boots and pull out the black heels she'd stored in the back of her closet. Way in the back.

Ugh. And she'd have to trade in her comfy socks for nylons. She spun around in the mirror. Maybe she could get away with high boots and black tights.

She picked up her tan overalls off the velvet-blue bench. Was she ready to hang these up for good?

Maybe, but not today. She slipped one arm out of the jacket and gave it a celebratory shake. "Much better."

"Char-liee! Come out of there right this second. I'm dying to see how the suit looks on you. You're trying on the plum one first, right?"

"Sorry, little arm. Back you go," she whispered and slid the jacket back on, tucking in the satin black top Gwen had also given her. "Don't you dare laugh." She opened the door.

Gwen's eyes widened. "Laugh? You look amazing! I knew that color would be just perfect with your skin tone. That purple is gorgeous." Her best friend placed her hands on Charlie's shoulders and spun her around. "I can't believe how great that jacket hangs on you." She inspected the cuffs. "Why, you aren't going to need any alterations at all."

Charlie hadn't thought about it being too long. "I guess that's a good thing, since I'll be wearing it on Monday. You really think I look professional?" she asked, her hesitation accentuated in every syllable.

Gwen made a face, reaching over and straightening out

the jacket. "You already are a professional."

"You know what I mean. I don't want to stick out like a sore thumb on the train ride." She sighed, glancing down at her wool socks again. "I feel like a misfit."

"You are certainly not. You, Charlie Dobbs, are going to fit right in with all the other New Yorkers. No, I take that back." She waved her hand high in the air. "You, my bestie, are going to shine as bright as the biggest star on Broadway."

"I don't need that kind of attention." Charlie took a step toward the dressing room. "Maybe I should go with one that's more basic. Doesn't everyone in New York wear all black anyway?"

That got a big ole head shake. Her best friend wasn't having it. "Plum is definitely your color. You look stunning, and you know what would make that outfit even better?"

"If I could do the interview via video conference and be comfortable from the waist down in my yoga pants and slippers with Jingles snuggled on my lap?"

"Ha, ha, ha. No. You will rock your *in-person* interview, and I've got a strand of pearls I picked up from this great vendor in the Garment District last month. It'll complete your interview outfit perfectly."

"My interview outfit," she repeated, staring at her reflection one last time. *I guess I'm doing this.* "Thank you." Charlie returned to the dressing room, changed back quickly into her overalls, and reemerged with the suit on its hanger. "I really love it."

"And I'm going to give you the Gwen Polaski friends and family discount." Gwen took the suit, sliding the string of pearls around the hanger. "And take off another fifty percent. Oh, and since purple is your color"—she reached for a headband and tossed it to Charlie—"maybe you could take off that old, wool thing once in a while and glam up your winter wear."

Charlie touched her black knit hat. "My mom made this, and you don't have to give me a discount on the suit." She had more than enough money in her savings account to pay for it. Besides, if she got the job, she was sure she'd be wearing it several times, so it was more or less an investment. But she couldn't wear it every workday. She gazed at the round racks throughout the boutique, full of all kinds of different tops and bottoms. She hadn't thought about it, but she'd have to get an entirely new wardrobe if she got the job. "I can pay full price."

Her bestie shook her head, hanging the outfit behind the counter. "I'm investing in your future. And solidifying a spot on your couch when I crash at your apartment next year during Fashion Week."

"Deal." Charlie checked the time on her phone. It was one p.m. on the nose. She had enough time to grab a quick lunch and head to the auto repair and body shop to install the part for Lillian's car. Spencer should be on his way back from Greenville by now.

"Do you have time to grab the Pizza & Pop Shop lunch

special? My treat." In addition to thanking her friend, she wanted to continue to pick Gwen's brain about pajama ideas. She had to have at least one decent one to present to Spencer when they met up to debrief this afternoon.

"A mouthwatering ricotta sausage slice and a large Cherry Coke? Twist my arm, why don't you?" Gwen grabbed her coat, gloves, and purse. "So, what else do you need to do to get ready for your interview?" she asked, while locking the front door.

"Practice. I found some standard interview questions on the internet and started rehearsing my responses this morning while rotating Titus Kelly's tires. I also wrote down key facts about the hotel on notecards to take with me for the train ride, studied the Barlow Automotive Designs website, and have my questions ready."

"Wow, all that in one morning. You've been productive."

She certainly had gotten some things done. Spencer's helping hand had given her the time she needed to hunker down and focus. She zipped up her jacket as they headed down the sidewalk. "It's nice that I have a Santa's helper today doing my errands."

"Oh, who?" Gwen asked. "Is it some type of volunteer program through the high school? How do I sign up for one?"

Charlie began to cross the street. "My helper is definitely not a teenager. It's Spencer," she said as if it was no big deal that a famous New York City fashion designer was running around town with her brown clipboard, crossing things off her to-do list. "He's delivering a part I need to install in Lillian Lathrop's car."

"Wait!" Gwen froze in the middle of the road and grabbed Charlie's arm. "Rewind that sentence back."

Charlie shoved the purple headband in her pocket and pulled her friend across the street. Lying motionless on hard gravel was not how she planned on spending her lunch break. "Mrs. Lathrop is leaving for Maine first thing in the morning. I've got to install a part and top off her fluids."

Gwen waved an exasperated hand in the air. "Further back."

"Oh, you mean, Spencer helping me." She smiled. "There's really no tea to spill here. We made a little deal— really, he insisted on it. He'd tackle some of the items on my to-do list to free up some time for me to come up with an idea for his jammies."

"Wow. I'm impressed."

"And thanks to him, I had the time to do all those things to get ready for my interview, including plotting out my commute into Grand Central Station."

"Ooh." Gwen touched Charlie's hand. "I always dreamed of commuting in and out of that train station. It always seemed romantic." She paused, adding, "I wonder if Spencer takes the train in."

"Doubt it," Charlie scoffed, heading down the sidewalk.

"I can pretty much guarantee that I will not be living anywhere remotely near him. Besides, if he doesn't drive his car, I imagine he calls a Lyft or Uber. I don't see him as a 'riding the train with the masses' type of guy."

Gwen gave a wink. "Maybe he has a fancy limo car service drive him around Manhattan."

"Now that wouldn't surprise me at all," Charlie agreed. The guy she'd met on The Vine in his fancy wool coat and cashmere scarf would probably be more apt to select a roomy leather backseat of a limo sedan than being squished in like a sardine between subway riders.

"Well, it'll be nice for you to have a friend in the city. Maybe he'll ask you out on a date."

"Very funny." Charlie grimaced and took a few more steps ahead, but Gwen didn't reply. She glanced over her shoulder. "You're joking, right?"

"What? You're single. He's single. You'd have a great time together."

"We don't know if he's single."

Gwen broke eye contact, tugging on her gloves.

"Or maybe we do?" Charlie narrowed her eyelids. "Do we know Spencer Carmichael's relationship status?"

Gwen shook her head no, but it morphed to a yes. "Okay, fine. I might have asked him when we were at Sheriff Thompson's stop on the crawl last night. In my defense, I'd had *three* Grinch hot chocolates."

Charlie proceeded down the street. Of course, Gwen

would immediately get the four-one-one on Spencer's relationship status. "Well, so what if he's single? He and I wouldn't hang out because we have zero in common."

"You're both from Brooks Bend."

"That doesn't mean we're going to date! I'm pretty sure from our limited interactions, I'm way too task orientated for his blood. He's . . . he's—" A vision of Spencer hovered over his Christmas cookie, meticulously piping the frosting, popped into her head.

Gwen was the one now waiting for a response, all smug lipped.

"He's not for me. I'm more interested in the type of guy who takes the train into work and gives up his seat immediately, even though it means he'll have to stand with his arm extended for the entire ride holding on to a filthy handgrip." She stopped in front of the door to the pizza shop that led up to her second-floor apartment. "One second." She pushed open the door to see an empty stairwell. "That's odd."

"What's odd?"

"Spencer was to drop off my Christmas tree by now, but it's not in there." The tree wasn't propped up next to her apartment door either.

"You had him pick up your Christmas tree?"

"Yeah, four hours ago."

"Interesting."

"Interesting how?"

Gwen opened the door to the Pizza & Pop Shop, holding it for Charlie. "Just seems like a pretty personal thing for a guy to do for you. Dare I say romantic?"

"Not even." Charlie rolled her eyes. "I needed to get my tree before Christmas but have had no time. He needs some holiday inspiration to jog his creativity. What better place but a Christmas tree farm. Win, win."

"Sure it's not you he needs?"

Charlie turned to her friend. "You really aren't going to let this go."

"I just think it's interesting timing and all that a handsome New Yorker who grew up in our small town is coming into your life right before you move to New York City. That's all."

*That's all. Uh-huh.* She needed to convince little Miss Cupid that there was no reason to launch her arrow. "Okay, first, I don't have the job yet. Second, he did not 'come into my life.' He crashed his car on The Vine. Third, even if I were interested in dating Spencer Carmichael, I am one hundred percent sure I am not that city boy's type."

"But you're going to be a city girl soon," she countered.

"Not an Upper West Side one."

Gwen pressed her lips together, appearing to put a pin in it—at least for the moment. They stepped up to the counter, the delicious aroma of fresh baked pizza swirling throughout the shop.

"Hi, ladies." Colin came through the swinging double doors that led to the kitchen, adjusting his apron.

"Colin, how's your knee doing?" Charlie asked.

"As good as new. Here's to another thirty years of running around this joint."

Gwen laughed. "Only thirty?"

He placed both hands on the counter and leaned in. "What can I get you both?"

"Two lunch specials with Cherry Cokes," Charlie replied. She and Gwen had been getting the same special since they were fifteen. She reached into her purse and pulled out her wallet.

Colin went to work, and in no time, set the large, ricotta-and-sausage slices onto two paper plates, heavily doused with Pop's secret seasoning, passed down by his grandpop. No one in town knew exactly what was in it, but, man, was it good. "So, Charlie." He reached for some fresh pizza dough, stretching it. "Do you know what time tonight you'll need help bringing up your tree?"

*How did Colin know about her tree?* "Um, no. I don't want you to aggravate your knee. I can handle it."

"Sure about that? Spencer seemed to think you might need an extra hand."

She cocked her head. "When did you talk to Spencer?"

That innocuous question got a huge belly laugh from Colin as he grabbed a roller and began rolling out the dough. "When haven't I is a better question. He's been calling every thirty minutes since I opened. Just hung up with him two minutes ago."

"The plot thickens," Gwen teased, her smile mischievous.

Charlie ignored her best friend. "What exactly has Spencer been asking you?"

"How wide is your entrance doorway?" He picked up the dough and tossed it in the air. "How tall are your ceilings? What's the general air quality of your apartment?"

Charlie's jaw tightened. *How tall are my ceilings? Air quality?* "He's supposed to be picking out a short four-foot tree, not one for Rockefeller Center."

"Well, the guy's committed, I'll give him that much. Can't wait to see it. If you need any help, give me a holler. If I can't do it, I can ask someone on my crew to assist you."

"Thank you. I will," she said flatly, following Gwen to a table. Had Spencer been at the Christmas tree lot this entire time?

She squeezed her eyes shut. *Oh, God. Did he forget to pick up Lillian's car part?* "Excuse me for a second," she said to Gwen and pulled out her phone, calling Spencer. When he didn't pick up, she sent him a quick text.

"Everything okay?" Gwen asked.

"No. Far from it." Charlie shook her head. "I should have never agreed to let Spencer help me. I asked him to pick up a performance part from an auto dealer in Greenville by noon, but it seems he was sidetracked." She let out a frustrated sigh and waited a few seconds for his text.

It didn't come. She called her dad.

"Dobbs Auto Repair and Body Shop."

"Hey, Dad. Just checking in. Did Spencer drop off the part for Lillian Lathrop's car?"

"No. Was he supposed to?"

"Yeah. All right. Thanks. I'll see you soon." Charlie hung up, trying to recall the conversation with Spencer. She'd specifically told him that the part needed to be picked up at noon.

She gripped her phone. Now Lillian wouldn't have her car to drive to Maine. Charlie needed to launch a plan B pronto, which meant getting a rental car for Lillian. "I'm sorry, Gwen. I've got to run. Can I stop by and grab the suit tomorrow?"

"Of course. Hey, go easy on Spencer. I'm sure he's just trying to help." She handed Charlie a paper plate. "Take your lunch."

"Thanks." Charlie grabbed her drink and took a bite of the slice while making her way outside. *Go easy, my eye.* The romance novel Gwen was trying to write with Spencer and Charlie as the main characters was going to turn into a small-town crime nonfiction because she was about to murder him.

# Chapter Ten

CHARLIE SEARCHED FOR the nearest car rental place, bringing the phone to her ear. In two minutes, she had a mid-sized four-door sedan reserved and permission from the manager to hook it up to her truck and tow it to Lillian's.

Making her way across town and up The Vine, it didn't take her long to pull up alongside the Christmas tree farm. Her temperature rose at the mere sight of Kristina's silver minivan in the parking lot.

Her fingers tightened around the steering wheel. *What on earth is he doing in there that took this long?* She yanked the wheel to the left, swerving into the lot. It should not take more than four hours to select and cut down a four-foot Christmas tree. This pact between them was over.

It would take two seconds to find Spencer, demand he turn over her to-do list, and call off this stupid agreement.

She had a reputation for providing quality and efficient service to her customers. They trusted her to get the job done on time. Let his reputation go down in flames—Spencer wasn't going to ruin hers.

She jumped out of the driver's side, slammed her truck door, and stormed past the hot chocolate and warm chestnuts truck, straight through the farm's main entrance, not bothering to do her yearly ritual of stopping for a minute to inhale the fresh pine air.

"Charlie. It's nice to see you," Joe Frier, the Christmas tree farm's owner and longtime friend of her parents, greeted her with a jolly smile.

"Hi, Joe. It's nice to see you." She glanced around at all the different sizes of pre-cut trees. Customers could either pick from the assortment or head into a sectioned-off area in the forest.

"You must be here to help chop down your tree."

*Help?!* Spencer shouldn't need her help if he'd only done what she asked. There was no way she should be swinging an axe right now. Not in her current mood. She narrowed her eyelids.

*On second thought.*

"Yes." She nodded. "I take it Spencer is still in the woods?"

That question got the same belly laugh Colin had given her earlier. "You could say that, but I think he's finally settled on the one."

"Terrific." Charlie pressed her lips together to avoid saying anything unflattering. "Could you tell me in which direction I will find him?"

Joe nodded, motioning over his shoulder. "Enter the

woods on the right and take the trail about thirty feet in and then head to your left. He was a few yards off the path the last time I checked. You should see him on the right."

"Thank you." She took a step forward.

"Charlie, how about sending someone else next year? Spencer's quite picky. I've already had to warn him three times that if he cuts it, he buys it. I've got enough in the pre-cut lot that I need to find homes for before next weekend."

"I'll do that. Thank you." She headed into the forest, her boots crunching on the snow-covered trail. This disastrous idea to help Mr. "I need to feel Christmas to get anything done" ended right now. Lillian was expecting to drive *her* car to Bangor, and now the sweet old woman had to get behind the wheel of an unfamiliar vehicle and drive six hours.

Charlie turned the corner to see Spencer on his knees with a tape measure. Her heart accelerated despite her anger. "Knock it off," she warned, causing Spencer to look up.

"Charlie!" He straightened and brushed pine needles off his jacket, then gloves. "What are you doing here?"

*What am I doing here?* She took a hit of the cold air. *Deep breaths. Deep breaths.* "Word around town is you've set up camp." *And I've come to break it down.*

He laughed, completely oblivious that she was about to put a kibosh on his merry mood. "Yeah, I spent more time here than I planned." He stepped closer, taking her gloved hand. "Just take a look at this place. Isn't it something? Truly breathtaking."

Under normal circumstances, she would wholeheartedly agree, but there was nothing normal about this holiday season.

He continued, not picking up on her silence. "At first, I thought it was going to be an impossible task with all these beauties to choose from. Did you know there are more than twenty different kinds of Christmas trees in here?" He shook his head, seemingly impressed. "Twenty."

He picked up the axe and motioned for her to follow him. "I had to get a tutorial from the owner, do some internet research on my phone, and work through some creative envisioning with my hands to determine angles, but I think I found your tree." He stopped talking and closed his eyes. "Can you smell it?"

Charlie shoved her hands in her jacket pockets. "Smell what?"

His smile stretched from Brooks Bend to Massachusetts. "Christmas."

*And here he goes again.* If she weren't completely ticked off, his breakthrough might be amusing, maybe even touching. "Um, Spencer. We need to ta—"

His eyes flew open. "You want to see your tree." He stopped in front a gigantic one, proudly motioning with his free hand. "Here it is."

Charlie glanced up, up, up at the tall, gorgeous Christmas tree with its dark-green needles, lightly dusted with snowflakes. She easily recognized it as a balsam fir. "That's definitely not my tree."

"What do you mean?"

"It has to be ten feet tall. It's way too tall for my living room."

"Actually, it's only a nine foot, give or take a couple of inches."

"I stand corrected."

"Okay, I can tell from your expression it wasn't what you were expecting, but Colin assured me there's a good fifteen feet from your floor to your ceiling. So you're good to go." He started to swing his axe.

"Wait!" she screamed, arms flailing.

He glanced up. "Did you want to do it?"

"No. No." She pinched the bridge of her nose. "Spencer, I appreciate your effort. I truly do, but this isn't going to work."

"It really isn't a problem, Charlie. I already measured the top of Kristina's minivan."

*Of course he had.*

"I can secure it to the top with Joe's assistance. I'll also carry the tree into your apartment and set it up. My dad can give me a hand if I need help, and if you need extra decorations, I'm sure my mother has some in our attic that she can lend you. That or I'll go buy some."

Wow. She stared at him, speechless. He'd really thought of everything. She'd be impressed if she weren't about to tow a rental clear across town to a customer expecting her own car back this afternoon.

That cold, hard reality helped tee up what needed to be said. "Spencer, while I appreciate your willingness to help with my to-do list and I'm genuinely happy that you've experienced the Christmas tradition of selecting a tree, any of the smaller ones would have been perfectly fine. Then you could have gotten Lillian's part."

"Lillian Lathrop's part, right." He set the axe down.

She put her hand up. "You don't have to bother. It's too late to get it now. The dealership is closed, and not only do I have to go and pick up a rental, I have to apologize to Lillian for not being able to fix her car in time." She paused for a beat to gather her thoughts. "I don't like letting my customers down, Spencer, which is why this agreement between you and me isn't working. Now that you've found Christmas, I'm sure you can design a great set of pajamas. Can I have my clipboard back?"

"Oh." His gaze met hers for a second.

*Is that all he has to say?* Clearly, she'd made the right decision calling this off. She held his gaze, not letting his ocean-blue eyes break her.

He finally bent down and picked up the clipboard from the ground, bushing snow off the back. "Here you go."

A knot formed in her stomach. She hated to be mean, but this really was for the best. "Thank you. I truly hope you come up with a new design soon." She turned and took a few steps down the trail, feeling like the grinchiest Grinch. *Just walk away, Charlie.*

"Hey, you said this morning you didn't need the part until two."

She stopped in place. She had said that. "Yes, but it needed to be picked up at noon."

"And it was. Hold on a second." He whipped out his phone from his jacket pocket. "Hey, Dad. Just checking that you dropped off the part to Fred Dobbs. You just left? Terrific. Thanks for doing that." He held the phone out. "I didn't want to lose focus on this mission, so I called in my squad. My father was looking for something to do, so I sent him for the part." He angled his screen in her direction. "I see you texted me earlier. Sorry about not seeing that. I was focused."

She swallowed. It was her turn to say a simple, "Oh."

He closed the distance between them, his eyes now twinkling, no doubt in triumphant celebration. "Seems like some of your 'get it done' attitude is rubbing off." He reached for her clipboard, taking it from her. "Now if you'll excuse me, I have a tree to cut down, and because I can see I haven't sold you on this beauty, I'll make sure it's a four-foot one." He brought up the axe. "I measured one that size that looked very nice not too far off the trail."

She stood dumbfounded.

"And, Charlie, about this afternoon, I'm going to pick up the paint you need, but my mom got on the phone while I was talking to my dad and asked if I'd run an errand for her. Could we go over your design ideas tonight at the Elfcapades instead of grabbing hot chocolate?"

What had just happened? Clearly Spencer was getting things done for her, yet she hadn't come up with one single design for him. "That would be great."

"Terrific. I'll see you then." He grinned and walked past her.

Wow. He'd really shown her. Suddenly, a question from her conversation with Gwen popped into her head. "Hey, Spencer."

"Yeah." He turned around, his gaze landing on hers, causing her knees to shake. She straightened.

"How do you get to work?"

"Excuse me?"

"What do you take? Your car, a taxi, Uber, luxury sedan, sleigh and reindeers?"

A line formed on his forehead. "Is this some type of auto mechanic assessment test?"

She shoved her hands in her jacket pockets. "Just curious."

"While the last one would make me the coolest uncle ever, I like to take the subway most days. Those parking garage entrance fees rack up when you go into the office five days a week. Why do you ask?"

"No reason." He started to leave again, and so help her, she was probably going to regret this, but she called out, "I'll take the tree."

Spencer spun around. "Which one?"

She nodded in the direction of the nine-foot balsam fir.

Spencer's eyes widened. "Really?"

"Yeah." She'd likely be sweeping up pine needles through New Year's Day, but he had spent more than four hours in the cold. "However, I'm totally taking you up on your offer of borrowing some of your mom's decorations. I don't have nearly enough ornaments for that size tree. Given you're way taller than me, I'm going to insist you help with stringing the lights and setting the star on top."

"You've got yourself a deal, Charlie Dobbs. I'm just going to let Joe know I'm cutting down this one and see if I can get some help carrying it out to the minivan." He looked over his shoulder. "Are Christmas lights negotiable?"

"No!" He was going to have to work through his trigger. Any tree of hers would be brightly lit.

"Okay, just thought I'd ask. See you tonight."

"See you." She watched him retreat down the trail, taking in his broad shoulders. Rarely did people surprise her.

She tipped her head. Never, actually.

But today, this man had. In spades.

# Chapter Eleven

"I THOUGHT TONIGHT was Six-Geese-a-Laying." Spencer swung his old ice hockey skates that he'd fished out of his parents' attic earlier over his shoulder and inspected the giant, orange-spotted giraffe his sister handed him from the backseat of the minivan. "I'm pretty sure this guy isn't part of any bird species."

Kristina emerged holding two brown teddy bears with giant red bows and gave them to Madeline and Ben before pulling out her own figure skates and a tiny blue elephant with fluffy ears. "Mom said that we were to bring stuffed animals to donate for our admission."

"And you decided to get this gigantic giraffe for me?"

She laughed and slid the van's door shut. "Well, there is quite a resemblance as far as height goes. What can I say? It reminded me of you. Lanky and goofy."

"I would have preferred a lion or a tiger. A scary one." He lowered himself to Madeline's eye level and gave a playful roar.

His niece's giggle filled the air. "You're so silly, Uncle Spencer."

"What's that grin for?" Spencer asked his sister as they walked through the parking lot toward the ice rink.

"Oh, nothing. It's just so nice to have my little brother here for Christmas." She winked. "Maybe it'll be an annual decision."

"Don't get your hopes up." If all went well, next year he'd be celebrating Christmas in Italy. Maybe the whole family could fly over.

He adjusted his grip on the giraffe. *One step at a time.* First, he needed to get the creative director residency, and that opportunity may have gone up in smoke this week with his pajamas.

They entered the ice rink area where a large crowd had gathered for tonight's sixth day of Elfcapades.

And apparently, this was the place to be. It was packed with bundled-up men, women, and children, many with ice skates slung around their shoulders.

Spencer took in the merriment all around them. True, he'd never experienced Elfcapades, but he had partaken in several Brooks Bend traditions growing up, including ice skating on this rink. It was good to see that some things never changed.

It wasn't strolling through Rockefeller Center or taking in an iconic holiday window display, but there was something about experiencing his small town's Christmas after all these years that lifted his spirits. He'd hardly given his pajama disaster or his canceled Bahamas trip a second thought today.

They joined the festivities, and he gave his niece an impromptu twirl to "Last Christmas" as Wham! blared through tall, black speakers. Along the ice rink's wall were several vendor tents—one being a make-your-own reindeer cocoa, which Ben was quick to point out—and stuffed animals were piled up in the middle of the rink.

He hoped to spot Charlie. Today had been fun. He'd completed the three tasks she assigned him, including delivering the tree to her apartment and talking to Colin about recruiting a couple of his employees to carry it up when Charlie got home.

Then he'd picked up the paint she'd needed. He'd wanted to run into her again this afternoon when he dropped it off at the auto repair and body shop, but she'd already left to deliver Lillian Lathrop's car.

His gaze moved toward the hot chocolate tent, catching Charlie walking up to it in her puffy black coat, a gold goose with a green ribbon around its neck in her arms.

He couldn't help but steal a long look. She looked incredibly beautiful with her blond hair tumbling around a purple hairband. His heart hummed along his rib cage.

Her gaze locked with his. His pulse quickened, and he gave her a short wave, trying to look as manly as he could, holding a ginormous stuffed giraffe.

He really should go over and apologize. She had every reason to be miffed. Though he enjoyed showing her that he could get things done without compromising his process, he should have told her as soon as she'd arrived at the Christmas tree farm that he'd asked his dad to pick up the part—better yet, he could have texted her the change of plans.

It hadn't been his intention to spend so much time in the woods, but each encounter with Charlie left him inspired. Witnessing her excitement as she shared her Christmas traditions with him last night and watching her pass out Christmas cookies this morning to the nursing home residents, one thing was clear: this holiday meant something to her. He'd been inspired to not just find any tree.

He wanted to find *her* tree.

A tree that she would enjoy stringing with popcorn while watching one of her favorite holiday movies. And, yes, it would also include some of his mom's Christmas decorations. He'd made good on that promise. After dinner, he'd gone up to the attic and brought down three boxes of ornaments his mom wasn't displaying this year.

A vision of him in Charlie's apartment helping her wrap strung popcorn around the tree popped into his head. They were both laughing after accidentally tangling a strand around their waists.

*Whoa.* He inhaled a deep, cold breath and patted his chest. *Easy, fella.* This Christmas crush he'd developed was silly and pointless. He'd be going home soon. Now wasn't the time to get all warm and fuzzy and develop feelings for a woman who wasn't going to be in his life past next Saturday.

But maybe that didn't have to be the case. Manhattan wasn't that far away. Maybe they could hang out in New York sometime. Perhaps he could invite her to go see a show. That was, if Charlie was into shows . . . or into him, for that matter. He cocked his head.

*Is she into me?*

She definitely wasn't this afternoon.

"Find who you're looking for?" Kristina piped up.

Reaching for Madeline, he brought her close and wrapped his arms around her, giving his niece a squeeze. "Everyone I'd be looking for is right here."

"Not everyone." His sister winked.

Leave it to Kristina to stir the pot. "Hey, kids. How about some reindeer cocoa before we hit the ice?" Just then, his phone vibrated inside his jacket pocket. "You go get fueled up, and I'll join you in a minute. I'll take a Rudolph with extra marshmallows."

His niece and nephew beelined for the tent, straight for Charlie, his sister close behind. He pulled out his phone. Roger was video calling him.

"Hey, Roger."

"Spencer." Roger beamed on screen, still sporting a suit and tie. "I see you're taking our advice and experiencing Christmas. Good for you. Are you outside?"

"Yes. I'm at my hometown's ice rink." He took a few steps away from the crowd. "Sorry about the noise."

"It sounds festive."

"It is. I'm about to have reindeer cocoa with my family and compete in the Six-Geese-a-Laying Contest for the town's coveted golden goose that, with any luck, will be placed on my mantel."

"I'm glad to see you in the Christmas spirit."

"So am I. It's been nice . . ." His voice trailed off.

This call was Roger making good on his word to check in on him in a couple of days. While there was no reason to tell him just yet about the deal he'd struck with Charlie, he could share that he'd brainstormed a couple of fun ideas while cutting down a Christmas tree, because he had.

But only if a backup was needed. He smiled over at Charlie, helping Ben decorate his hot chocolate with sprinkles. *She'll come through.*

"I've got some ideas, Roger, that I think you'll love and so will the investors. I'm confident I'll have a new design for you next week."

"I look forward to seeing it, and I've got a great present for you, Spencer. The Accettare deal is a go. We got word a few hours ago from Milan. Start packing your bags and brushing up on your Italian. The creative director residency is yours. You'll leave right after the new year."

SPENCER'S JAW DROPPED. Did he hear Roger correctly? "You

chose me? Even after this week?"

Roger's face softened. "Spencer, it was never a question which of our designers would represent Warwick's. You are going to be our first resident, working side by side with some of fashion's greatest talent for an entire year. You'll have your own line of sustainable, eco-friendly couture that will be exclusive to Warwick's."

"Oh wow." Spencer moved the phone slightly down to see Ben reaching for Charlie's hand. His dream to branch out from sleepwear, but in a meaningful way, was coming true. "That's uh . . . really terrific," he muttered, bringing the phone back up. "Amazing news."

Roger continued, seeming oblivious to Spencer's flubbing. "I'll ask the public relations department to generate a press release ASAP announcing the partnership and your new role."

"Thank you for this news, Roger, and for everything. I'm humbled by your confidence in me to introduce Warwick's first eco-friendly line." He said goodbye and slid his phone back into his pocket.

*I'm moving to Italy.*

He placed his palm flat against his cheek. He'd prayed for this moment for months.

*I'm moving to Italy!*

Working in arguably the crown jewel of the fashion industry among all that thriving talent and all those textures was any serious designer's dream come true. The last eight months had been about getting closer to this goalpost.

He walked back toward the hot chocolate tent. Charlie was showing off the golden goose to Ben and Madeline.

"Hey." Charlie handed him a hot chocolate. Lodged in the whipped cream were two chocolate slivers for eyes and a cherry nose. "One Rudolph hot chocolate for Brooks Bend, Connecticut's most famous native."

"Thank you." He chuckled and took a sip. The cold whipped cream touched his nose.

"So, I assume that's the coveted Christmas goose." He ran the back of his finger across his nose and nodded down to the stuffed thing sitting on the bench table next to Ben.

"That it is." She adjusted her skates around her shoulder, retrieved the goose, and hoisted it up. "It's a beauty, isn't it?"

"Hmm, I was envisioning something a bit more mallard regal."

She tugged gently on the green velvet ribbon around its neck. "Don't listen to him, Brookie. I think you're beautiful."

He lifted an eyebrow. "Brookie?"

"Yes, Brookie. I was actually just going to keep her on my mantel, but people like to see her once a year."

"Brookie, I think you're really going to enjoy your new view of Central Park."

Charlie held the goose tight. "She prefers her spot high atop Main Street."

"I'm sure she does, and speaking of your apartment, I

was thinking maybe I could bring over Mom's decorations tomorrow night and help you trim your tree. Perhaps we could grab some Chinese takeout and make an evening of it."

"Um . . ."

*Oh, man.* Was that too forward? "I mean, that is if you don't have other plans." Maybe she was doing something else tomorrow night. For all he knew, she could be dating someone.

"Uh, no. Um . . . I mean, I don't have plans."

"Great. It's a date."

"Attention, skaters," Mr. Skillman, the retired gym teacher and tonight's emcee, quieted the crowd. "The Six-Geese-a-Laying race will begin in five minutes. Please make sure you've handed your donated stuffed animal to one of our volunteers wearing reindeer antlers to take to the animal pit." Mr. Skillman continued into the microphone, "And Charlie Dobbs, please hand over the Golden Goose."

Out of nowhere, a volunteer came up to them, snatching Brookie from Charlie's arms before taking Spencer's giraffe.

"I guess it's time to go win that goose." He nodded to an empty bench. "Shall we go lace up?"

"As reigning champ for the last three years, I have no intention of giving up Brookie." Charlie followed him, and they took a few minutes to put on their skates.

"I admire your determination." His voice turned serious. "Hey, can we talk a minute about today?"

"Sure."

"I'm really sorry that I stressed you out. It wasn't my intention to upset you. I only wanted to help." He paused. "Maybe I went a little overboard on the tree."

"There's no need to apologize." She tightened her skate laces and placed her boots under the bench. "I overreacted, but it all worked out. Lillian was none the wiser when I dropped off her car this afternoon." She let out a sigh. "Now don't get a big head from what I'm about to admit, but the tree is really superb."

"I knew it would look great. It's the perfect height and width next to your fireplace without blocking out the natural light you get from your living room window, isn't it?"

She gave him some serious side-eye, but admitted, "It's perfect. Your research was spot-on."

"Yes!" He made a fist and pumped the air.

"And I'm going to have a word with Colin for telling a total stranger such specific details about my apartment."

"Total stranger?" He waggled his eyebrows.

"Somewhat stranger."

"Maybe we can work on that."

Her cheeks got noticeably brighter. He bent down and slid his loafers under the bench next to her boots. "Do you think it's safe to leave our shoes here?" he asked.

"I think it's okay. It is Brooks Bend, after all."

"Right. Good point." They made their way to the ice. "Why do I feel like I might break an ankle?" His legs wobbled as his blades slanted.

"I take it, it's been a while since you took a spin around a rink." Charlie pushed off and glided in front of him, doing a half turn so that she was skating backward.

"Show-off."

"No, this is showing off." She skated a few feet away and turned in a circle, crossing her arms as she spun around and around.

"Auto mechanic by day, figure skater by night, I see. You continue to surprise me."

She came out of her spin. "Okay, so do you remember playing hot potato when you were a kid?"

"Vaguely," he said, focusing on staying upright. The last thing he wanted was to face-plant in front of the woman he was trying to impress.

And let's face it, that's exactly what he was trying to do.

"Well, this first competition is a variation of the game. After the countdown, we'll all skate to the stuffed animal pit and search for a goose."

"Ah . . . I get it . . . Geese a-laying."

She smiled and continued. "There are twenty hidden in the pile. Those who find one then advance to the next round, which is the hot potato round. The object is to be holding one of six geese with a candy cane zipped into its belly when the music stops."

They completed their first lap, his confidence in his skating ability improving. "So this is more a game of chance that you've won three years in a row?"

"The first and second rounds, yes, but the third and final round takes a certain type of skill."

"What happens after I get a goose with a candy cane?"

She smirked, spinning backward. "You'll see. Good luck."

"Okay, skaters, please make your way to the wall," Mr. Skillman announced. Charlie skated over to Madeline and Ben, giving each a high five.

"That's my old soccer coach." Spencer came up next to her and gave him a wave. "I've so got this in the bag."

"He's not going to help you." Charlie laced her fingers in front of her and stretched.

"Want to make this whole thing more interesting if you and I advance to the third round?"

She glanced over, lifting an eyebrow. "What do you have in mind?"

"Should we both end up with a candy cane, winner between you and me buys the other a drink." He nodded in the direction of the tents. "I see this place is serving adult beverages."

"Deal." She bent her knees in a speed skater stance. "I'll take a toasted almond cocktail with my golden goose, and make sure they swirl the rim in crushed graham crackers."

"All right, everyone," Mr. Skillman began. "On the count of three, race to the stuffed animals and find the twenty geese. One. Two. Three!"

Spencer pushed off his blades straight for the plush pile. He began searching for a goose, moving every panda bear, koala, and kitten aside and out of his way.

Charlie came up beside him. "Here you go." She tossed him a dolphin.

"You trying to distract me isn't working." He threw it back into the pile.

"Got one!" Charlie stood, flashing a feathery goose. "You could forfeit now."

"Never. There are plenty still left in here." He sifted through the pile. He wasn't leaving this animal pit until he found one.

"UNCLE SPENCER, CHARLIE. We both got a goose." Madeline and Ben skated up to Charlie, each proudly holding their stuffed animal.

"Good job, kids." Amused, Charlie nodded at Spencer, still desperately searching for a goose. "Looks like your uncle might be having some trouble. Maybe you could help him out?"

The kids began to search the animals just as Gwen skated up holding a goose.

"Well, look at you. In it to win it, I see."

"Since the Belle & Beau is sponsoring the drink tent, I thought I'd get into the action." Gwen petted her goose.

"This would be way better if the winner received more than that tacky Golden Goose. No offense to Brookie, but I think I'll throw in a free outfit for the winner." Her gaze zoomed into the animal pit, and Spencer trying to make the case to his niece and nephew that the duck he was holding counted. "He's really trying."

Charlie couldn't help but chuckle. The sleepwear designer certainly wasn't giving up. "We have a little side bet going on if we both advance to the third round."

"Oh, really? What kind of bet?"

"Loser between us buys the winner a Christmas drink."

"I see . . ." was all Gwen said, but with a telltale smirk that stopped that sentence from drifting into utterly ridiculous territory.

"Don't get any ideas. It's an innocent drink, probably on one of the benches with everyone around. It doesn't even look like it's happening because he's not going to make it to the second round."

"Sure he is. Hey, Carmichael. Heads-up," Gwen called out. He spun around just in time to catch the goose that Gwen hurled straight for him. "Sorry."

"Thanks, Gwennie." He skated over to his niece and nephew, showing off his goose.

Charlie shook her head. "That's cheating."

"I shouldn't be playing anyway since I'm a sponsor. Besides . . ." Gwen gave Charlie's arm a squeeze, causing Charlie to bobble. "It also ensures my best friend gets to enjoy a tasty Christmas cocktail with a handsome man this year and not go home alone."

Charlie protested. "I never went home alone. I had Brookie."

"Uh-huh. Have fun on your date. I hear it might even snow later. Now, how perfect would that be for the two of you?" Gwen winked, spun around, and began to skate backward.

"Oh, by the way, your hair looks awesome tonight. Glad you retired the hat. Purple's definitely your color."

Charlie touched the headband. Okay, sure. She'd paid a little more attention to her hair when getting ready. It wasn't like she knew Spencer was going to invite her to have a drink with him.

Her pulse quickened. But she did know he'd be here.

She began to skate around the rink, humming to "Baby It's Cold Outside" coming from the live band that had just begun to play, and exchanging smiles with Spencer as he skated by with Madeline and Ben.

*What in the world are you doing?* She ignored that question asked by the more sensible, cautious angel on her shoulder. There was nothing wrong with a little holiday flirting. Plus, thanks to Gwen's sleuthing, he was single.

And she was too. Her gaze moved over to Evan hand in hand with Jillian, looking like the perfectly dressed couple in a Rockefeller painting in their matching red coats gliding along the ice, and having a hard time picturing what she and

Evan must have looked like together.

The "hot goose" race began with twenty participants flying around the rink, tossing their geese. She tossed her goose to Nicole, an elementary school teacher, and caught one from Zach, who ran the local animal shelter.

When the music stopped, she held her breath and turned her goose around, unzipping its belly. A red-and-white striped candy cane was tucked inside.

She spun around to see Spencer tossing her a huge grin, flashing a candy cane before Madeline tugged for his attention.

Her heart began to gallop. *I'm having a Christmas drink with Spencer Carmichael!*

# Chapter Twelve

"I'M THINKING THAT gingerbread ale is going to hit the spot." Spencer sat down and next to Charlie, setting his goose next to hers. "Just so you have my order for later."

She pulled her foot out of the skate, shoving it into her boot. "Hate to break it to you, but the next round involves knowing everything about Christmas." She gave her laces a triumphant tie. "And I mean everything."

"I know a thing or two about Christmas." He pulled off his skates and slipped on his shoes.

"Uh-huh." She picked up her goose. "That it's on December twenty-fifth doesn't count."

He chuckled and tucked the candy cane he'd been holding back inside his goose. "Putting aside the fact that a significant number of people in the country are probably wearing last year's S.C. Christmas pajamas, as of today, I know a few more things." His eyes twinkled. "Take, for instance, there's more than one kind of Christmas tree growing up on top of The Vine—twenty, in fact. I also know that everyone over eighty in this town loves a frosted sugar cookie for breakfast when it's delivered by their favorite auto mechanic."

Her insides warmed at that comment. "Flattery won't get you the golden goose."

They made their way to the tent where a crowd had gathered. She sized up this year's competition that included Evan, Jillian, Sheriff Thompson, and Rebecca Hemsworth, a former classmate who was home for the holidays.

Charlie focused her attention on the giant red-and-green wheel that she and her mother had helped Mr. Skillman's wife, Evelyn, put together five years ago. Her heart melted, thinking back to how excited her mom had been on the eve of the inaugural event, Velcroing categories on the wheel while munching on caramel popcorn.

Her mom hadn't been feeling well that night, but she'd made the effort. She knew it was her last Christmas. She'd passed away two months later.

Charlie closed her eyes to prevent the tears from flowing as Spencer read the words off the wheel.

"Holiday Laughs. The Right (X-Mas) Stuff. Christmas in the Air."

Her lids flew open. She gave his arm a teasing pat. "Just close your eyes and inhale."

"All right, everyone." Mr. Skillman began to run through the instructions. "For those who are new, these next two rounds test your Christmas memory and sensory skills."

Charlie turned to Spencer, lowering her lashes, which she hoped came off as playful and not antagonizing. "You could duck out now. Exit stage right."

"Nope." Spencer shook his head just as his sister, niece, and nephew joined them. He ruffled up his nephew. "Let's do this, Christmas."

Mr. Skillman began the game. Evan had been randomly selected to begin. Her ex gleefully stepped up to the wheel and gave it a good spin. When it finally landed on Holiday Laughs, he chose to take on Sheriff Thompson and Spencer, passing over Charlie's "I triple-dog dare you" eyebrow quirk.

"Good luck, Spencer. You got this," Kristina cheered, but then turned to Charlie. "He has no chance."

"I heard that." Spencer made his way to the front. Mr. Skillman took a moment to brief the three.

"Well, frost my sugar cookie and call it a Christmas miracle."

Charlie spun around to see that Gwen, holding onto a frosted caramel apple ale, had made it to the adult beverage tent. "What are you talking about?"

"Your Christmas present squaring off with your Christmas past. How apropos. My money's on the tall one not wearing that dorky turtleneck."

"Would you stop?" Charlie bit down a laugh at the mention of Evan's signature attire. She had firsthand knowledge that folded neatly in his dresser were twenty more just like the red one he was sporting tonight. She lowered her voice so that Kristina wouldn't overhear. "Spencer is *not* my present, real-time or otherwise."

"Maybe you didn't ask Santa for him." Gwen winked. "But he's here now."

"Okay, gentleman," Mr. Skillman began. "The goal is to outdo each other in the holiday comedy category. Last one to be able to name a Christmas movie that makes us chuckle wins. Mayor Hertzberg, you can begin."

"*Home Alone*," Evan proudly started.

"He kind of looks like that kid," Gwen quipped.

Charlie gave her a nudge, and they watched as round after round, Spencer actually held his own, naming *Christmas Vacation* and *Four Christmases*, and a couple of old movies she hadn't seen, including *Shop Around the Corner*. Sheriff Thompson was stumped and sidelined after the second round.

"I'm impressed," she said to Kristina.

"This is actually a good category for him. Growing up, Spencer would watch movies in his room twenty-four seven while drawing. Even on Christmas morning, Mom struggled to get him to come downstairs. She finally had to remove all electronics from his room."

"Really?"

Kristina nodded. "His first pajama design was inspired by *It's a Wonderful Life*. Do you have that pair? Light blue with bells and wings?"

Charlie stared at her blankly. Now didn't feel like the time to admit she mainly wore holey T-shirts and yoga pants to bed. "No, but maybe I can look them up on the internet."

Charlie tilted her head. If Spencer had watched Christmas movies feverishly growing up, why was it so difficult for him to tap into the holiday spirit when he needed it most? Maybe because it'd been tied to his commercial success all these years, he'd lost touch with the magic of Christmas.

"*Die Hard!*" Evan screamed out, gathering his composure. "Some may argue it's not, but it's definitely a Christmas one."

Charlie shook her head. Maybe, but funny was a big stretch . . .

Mr. Skillman turned to Spencer. "What'cha got for us?"

"Hmm, another Christmas movie." Spencer placed a hand on his forehead, but seemed to be at a loss. "Just a second, Coach."

Evan did a celebratory jig, doing a heel-toe with his boot.

Charlie rolled her eyes. Squaring off against Evan wasn't a big deal. She was pretty sure she'd be able to whoop him. Still . . . her gaze settled on Spencer. It'd be fun to face off against the sleepwear designer should they both make it through.

Charlie bit back a grin. It was time to knock Evan out of this round, and she knew just how to do it. She placed her hand on top of her head. *Look at me.* She willed Spencer to glance her way. She was about to lose hope when he finally did.

She pointed at Evan, lowering her finger all the way down.

His lips turned into a wide smile.

*Message received!*

"It's okay if you can't think of one last movie," Evan said, puffing up his chest and extending his hand. "Nice effort."

"*Elf,*" Spencer said, smiling at Charlie. "Best Christmas comedy ever. Final answer."

The crowd erupted in applause that continued after Evan could not think of another movie to take the win.

Charlie made her way to the front to congratulate Spencer, but not before Rebecca stepped up and high-fived him. "I love that movie. It's so funny." Rebecca flashed her huge smile up at Spencer while Jillian consoled Evan.

"You know," Jillian started, ignoring that Charlie had joined the group. "You two should come over some night next week and watch it with us. We'd love to have you over for dinner, wouldn't we, dear?"

"Uh, sure." Evan didn't seem quite so eager to welcome Spencer back to his home.

"It's settled." Jillian beamed. "Do you both like Mexican? Evan makes the best enchiladas. I'll call you both tomorrow with the details."

Charlie shoved her hands in her jacket pockets and turned to the wheel, pretending to be preoccupied with it and not the double date being arranged in front of her. The words went blurry as she tried to tune out the conversation. *You need to get a grip.* Who Spencer spent his time with in

Brooks Bend shouldn't matter.

She took a deep breath. For some reason, it did.

Suddenly, she felt a hand on her arm. She glanced up to see Spencer smiling down at her. "Hey, good luck."

"Thanks," she said, feeling far less confident than she did earlier. Her chest hardened as she took her place between a smug Jillian and an ecstatically bubbly Rebecca to compete in the next round.

Even if she won, going home with Brookie now felt like a consolation prize.

# Chapter Thirteen

S PENCER MADE HIS way back into the crowd, stopping next to Gwennie as Jillian spun the wheel. Her spin landed on The Right (X-Mas) Stuff.

"All right, ladies." Coach Skillman handed each a red velvet Christmas stocking. "You have thirty seconds to feel around your stocking. The contestant who can name correctly the most items inside advances to the final round."

"I hope Charlie wins," Gwennie said.

"She's really attached to that golden goose, huh?"

That got a snort out of Gwennie. "Yeah, but also Jillian's always trying to one-up her. That woman makes it her recreational pastime to get Charlie's goat."

"She's pretty good at it, I take it?" He suspected the impromptu movie-night invitation Jillian had conveniently left Charlie out of, despite her standing right there, was more about ruffling Charlie's feathers and not setting him up with Rebecca.

The art curator was nice and all, but he wouldn't be going to the mayor's house to watch *Elf* anytime soon. He grinned at Charlie now squishing her stocking's toe. His pulse ticked up. She's who he wanted to spend his remaining time in Brooks Bend getting to know. "Jillian doesn't ease up during the holidays?"

"No, but Charlie's got me watching her back." She touched his arm. "Speaking of having someone to look out for her, my girl is going to need a friend when she moves to New York City."

His jaw flew open. *Wait. What?* He couldn't possibly have heard Gwennie correctly. "Charlie's moving to Manhattan?"

She nodded. The cold air hadn't impacted his hearing.

"When?"

"Hopefully, in the new year. Listen, don't tell her I told you. She'd kill me. It's just . . ." She shrugged a shoulder. "It'd be nice if she knew a familiar face while she's getting settled. Maybe someone she could meet up with for coffee." She gave him a wink. "Or maybe take her to a nice dinner at one of those trendy NYC eateries."

"Uh. Yeah, I could do that," he said, still a bit rattled by that breaking news. "If she moves to the city, that is." He stared forward, breathing in the cool air.

So the automotive design job Charlie had mentioned this morning was in Manhattan.

*Well, this is lousy timing.* Charlie was potentially moving to New York City at the same time he was exiting it.

"Good job, Jillian." Coach Skillman's praise interrupted his thoughts. "You have surpassed Rebecca's four items.

Okay, Charlie. To beat Jillian, you need to name six items in your stocking correctly. Are you ready?"

"Yes. It was definitely challenging but"—Charlie handed over her stocking—"I believe it contains lip balm, an orange, a perfume bottle, one candle, a wine bottle opener." She paused, her smile growing wide. "And definitely a monkey wrench, which I'm excited about, because I could use a new one."

Coach Skillman did the honors of pulling out all the stocking stuffers Charlie had listed, building a little suspense on the last one, but nevertheless, pulled out a monkey wrench. "Congratulations, Charlie Dobbs. You'll advance to the final round and the chance to hold on to your title."

A miffed Jillian stepped into the crowd, joining Spencer. "Of course she'd know that there was a monkey wrench in her stocking. That's hardly fair."

"There's always next year," he offered, masking his amusement.

"Uh-huh," Jillian mumbled under pressed lips. He stepped forward, but she caught his arm. "Take her down."

Wow. He glanced down at the clutch she had on him. So much for Christmas spirit. "I'll do my best."

"And afterward, let's grab a drink." She spun around. "I'll go get Rebecca and Evan. We'll meet you in the tent."

"Sorry. I've already made plans with Charlie for this evening, but thank you." He left Jillian with her mouth wide open, grinning as he made his way to the front next to

Charlie. "Fancy meeting you here."

"Charlie, since you are the reigning champ, the wheel is yours." Coach Skillman stepped to the side. "Give it a good yank."

Seconds later, her spin landed on Christmas Is in the Air. Evelyn approached, holding a red bandana. She asked Spencer to squat down while she placed it over his eyes and tied the back. "I didn't see this coming," he muttered.

"You'll be fine," he heard Charlie say. "Just take a deep breath and relax."

Easier said than done. He stood awkwardly in the dark until the coach announced that the round was starting and instructed him to take a big whiff.

The clean scent of fresh pine filled his lungs.

"Okay, Spencer. This contest is all about identifying Christmas scents. Tell us what you smell. You get two whiffs."

He took another whiff, pretty sure he had this one. "Is it a Christmas tree?"

"Correct."

He waved his arms in celebration, accidentally hitting something soft—strike that—someone soft, based on Evelyn's yelp. "I'm so sorry."

"Charlie. You're next. And, Spencer, you can slide up your blindfold while Charlie's guessing, so as not to accost my wife again. Charlie, same goes for you when it's Spencer's turn."

He didn't need that instruction twice. He slid it up just in time to see Charlie taking a whiff of a bowl filled with chestnuts.

And darn, she looked cute all blindfolded, with loose curls over her shoulder and her nose in the bowl.

"Is it roasted chestnuts?" she asked.

"Correct." Coach Skillman made mention that the chestnuts were on sale in the next tent with proceeds going to the after-school library program.

The second round continued with his guessing eggnog correctly, while she easily knew the scent of gingerbread.

He slid his blindfold over his eyes for the third round, inhaling something with cinnamon and some sort of fruity scent he didn't recognize. "Is it a fruitcake?" It was the only thing he could think of that had cinnamon in it. His grandma used to make one every year, and she'd let him sprinkle the cinnamon on the top.

"That is correct."

Spencer removed his blindfold to see Evelyn holding a slice of fruitcake, but he passed when she offered him a bite.

"All right, Charlie." Mr. Skillman picked up the golden goose from the table it was displayed on, showing it off to the crowd. "You need to guess this to advance to a tiebreaker."

She smiled at Spencer and then slid her blindfold back on. "Let's do this, Christmas."

He gazed over at the cocktail tent. He'd make a beeline

over there once she won.

"Okay, Charlie. Take a whiff."

Spencer watched as Coach Skillman put a bowl of snow under Charlie's nose. She took a sniff. "This is kind of hard. Is there anything in there?"

Maybe he could give her a hand like she did in his round. With one finger to his lips and a nod to Evelyn, he scooped up some snow from the bowl, coating Charlie's nose.

She stood silent for a second and then another. "It can't be. This is all wrong." She whipped off the blindfold, her face flushed.

And if he weren't mistaken, horrified. "I'm so sorry." He wiped his hand on his jeans. "I was trying to help."

"Uh, right." She swiped her nose. "Congratulations, you win. Thank you, Mr. Skillman, for emceeing. I've got to go."

He watched her bolt through the crowd. *What just happened?*

Whatever he'd done, it was clear he'd upset Charlie. *Good going, man.* He politely let his former coach do the honors of handing him the golden goose before joining Gwennie.

"Hey."

"Hey." She held up her beer bottle and toasted him. "Cheers to getting that hideous thing out of Charlie's apartment."

He laughed. "I'm not sure it'll look any better in mine.

Do you know why she tore out of here? If this really means a lot to her, she can keep it."

"It's not about the goose."

"It isn't?" He cocked his head. What was he missing? "Is she super competitive?"

"Well, yes, but that's not it. She has a thing with snow. It kinda freaks her out." She took a long sip of her ale.

"Really?" Weird, given her line of work. She didn't seem to have a problem with it the other night when she towed him off The Vine.

It was supposed to snow tonight. Was she afraid to drive in it? "I would think her vehicle would do quite well on icy roads."

Gwennie snorted out a little of the ale. "That's not the issue. Here's the scoop. It was snowing the first time her mother told her father she loved him. Her mom had this fairy-tale notion that it would be snowing the moment Charlie found true love too."

His lips parted. *Love?* "Uh . . ."

"Don't worry." Gwennie gave his shoulder a pat. "I doubt she was thinking it was happening tonight. She embarrasses super easily, which you probably gathered from her presentation at the mayor's house."

"I did notice that . . ." His voice trailed away as he looked off in the direction of the bench they'd sat on earlier. It was empty.

"That, and pretty much the entire town knows about her

mother's prediction. We keep an eye on the weather in these parts, and not just for slippery roads." She winked and nodded in the direction of the town's square. "I think you'll find Charlie over there."

"Thanks." He didn't really understand the snow premonition, but if he'd embarrassed her, he wanted to apologize. He said a quick goodbye and found Kristina to let her know he'd walk home. Making his way to the town's square, he spotted Charlie sitting alone on a bench in front of the enormous Christmas tree. His breath caught as he closed the distance between them.

"Mind if I join you?"

She glanced up, her face red. "Sure." She nodded toward the golden goose. "Congratulations."

He sat down and rested it on his lap. "Brooklyn's much heavier than I realized. She'll make a great paperweight."

She rolled her eyes at his name change and reached over, petting the goose. "That fruitcake guess was quite something. I don't think I would have gotten it on smell alone."

"My grandmother made it every year when I was growing up."

He set Brookie down between them. "I'm sorry about . . ." How should he apologize about freaking a woman out with snow? Maybe it was better to not bring it up. "You should have won."

"No. You did fair and square." She rested her hand on the goose. "I'm sure you will give her a good home."

"You could come visit," he said, adding, "Rumor has it this bird may have been heading south anyway."

She shook her head. "Since my dad and Dee Dee aren't here tonight to blab that news, let me guess. You heard it from Gwen."

"Does she not go by Gwennie?"

"Not since she was seven."

"Ahh, I'll remember that next time, and, yeah, she did mention it because she wants you to be happy."

"I know. She always looks out for me."

"She's a good friend." Maybe he could be one too. He wouldn't be there when she arrived, but he could give her some pointers. "So, the job you're interviewing for is in New York City?"

She nodded.

"Well, I admire the courage that must take to start a career so different than the one you're currently doing. Plus, that foot-massager floor mat you made is the real deal."

That got a big smile. "Well, thanks. I still need to ace the interview and be offered the job before I can start boxing up my apartment. I'm kind of nervous." She bit her lip. "And by kind of, I mean scared out of my mind."

"I could give you some tips." He lightly bumped his shoulder against hers.

"Uh-huh."

Okay, he one hundred-percent deserved the skeptical side-eye she was giving him. "Don't worry. I won't suggest picturing anyone dressed up as an elf. I promise." He chuckled, then added, "Although, I do appreciate your help tonight by reminding me that I said the mayor looked like a very tall one."

"Yeah, Evan should have been kicked out for that *Die Hard* answer."

"It is a Christmas movie. I'll give him that."

"It's so not."

That disagreement seemed to lift her mood and gave him the courage to ask another question needling him. "Okay, this is probably none of my business, but what did you ever see in that dude?"

"That's a very good question." She adjusted her head-band over her ears. "His mom would often bring her car into the shop for regular oil changes, and she'd always talk up her son who was in college, her son who was in law school, her son who passed the bar exam and was moving back to Brooks Bend. This went on for years. Then one day, she sent Evan in for her oil change. After I was done, he asked me for coffee. We started dating shortly after."

She continued. "We didn't last long, though, not even a year. Truthfully, Jillian's a way better match—the royal couple of Brooks Bend."

"Royal couple," he repeated and chuckled. "That's one way of putting it."

She sighed and pulled up the zipper on her puffy coat. "One time, I raced across town for a special ribbon-cutting ceremony for the animal shelter's new medical-center wing. It was a big deal due to a large donation. I hadn't had time to change, but since I was wearing red overalls and it was the holidays, I thought it would be fine. We were all gathered for a press photo. I was holding the sweetest gray tabby."

Charlie sporting a black turtleneck and cute red overalls. She must have looked adorable. "Something happen?"

"Evan asked me to hand over the cat to one of the shelter's staff and step aside."

*Ass!*

"We broke up not long after." She shook her head, but brightened instantly. "I did adopt the cat. Her name is Jingles, and I just love her to pieces."

"Sounds like you had a good Christmas after all."

"Maybe so." She laughed, but then grew serious. "About this Christmas. Spencer, there's something I really need to tell you."

That didn't sound good. Neither did the worry in her eyes. "What's that?"

"I don't have one idea for your jammies—I mean, pajamas. I'm so sorry."

Relief washed over him. That admission he could handle. "It's okay."

"No, it's not. You did all those wonderful things to help me today." She blew out a frustrated breath. "And I don't have one decent idea for you."

"It's fine. Really. It's not a big deal."

"You're not worried?"

"Not at all. It's not easy. Trust me. Why don't you do this: write down everything that comes to mind when you think of Christmas. Bounce my red rubber ball in your free hand while you're doing it. We'll then go over the list tomorrow night while we're decorating your tree."

She narrowed her eyes. "That seems like cheating."

"It's called collaboration—a Christmas one. I think we've proven we do it quite well."

It appeared her cheeks were getting redder.

"You know, you really don't need me." She cocked her head in the direction of the ice rink. "You did completely fine tonight all on your own."

He grinned. Maybe true, but she was inspiring him with each and every encounter. "I like our arrangement."

"Well"—she laced her fingers and gave her arms a good stretch—"I should probably go check on my tree. Make sure Jingles hasn't knocked it over."

"Aw, the infamous Jingles. I'm looking forward to meeting her."

"You know it's not going to be enchiladas and *Elf* at the mayor's mansion."

He couldn't help but laugh. "Promise?"

"I'll see you tomorrow." She smiled and nodded down to the goose. "Congratulations again. Make sure you take real good care of Brookie."

"You can see her anytime," he called out as she headed

out of the town's square onto Main Street. It took only a few minutes for Charlie to disappear into her apartment building.

Sure, they didn't get to that drink, but tonight had ended pretty near perfectly.

He turned back and picked up the goose. Suddenly, his nose felt something wet. He glanced up as snowflakes gently fell from the starlit sky.

Maybe the "L" word was far away or maybe it wouldn't happen, but this new hum in his heart had to mean something. He tilted his head back and closed his eyes, letting the snowflakes coat onto his nose and eyelashes.

Let it snow. Let it snow. Let it snow.

# Chapter Fourteen

*C*ANDY CANES. *SILVER bells, red ribbons.* Charlie dropped the red rubber ball on her kitchen table, picking it up, repeating the motion. She'd been at it for an hour and had a page full of words that came to mind when she thought of Christmas, but none had sparked a really clever jammies idea.

She reached for Spencer's iPad and tapped on his prototype folder, eyeing what looked like a fun design. The top was a perfectly wrapped present with "Santa, I was good this year" in cursive below it. The red bottoms displayed items she suspected could be in the box. Jewelry, mittens, wireless headphones, and even a puppy ran down the legs.

It was kinda fun. *I wonder why it didn't make the cut.*

Jingles jumped up on her dining room table and made an unsuccessful attempt for the red ball before Charlie swept it away. "How about you don't inject your claws into Spencer's ideation ball?" She gave Jingles' fur behind her ears a good scratch that always made the feline purr. "Let's get out some of your toys."

She went to the cat's toy bowl on her bookcase, pulled

out the little jingle bell-felt balls she'd purchased for her last Christmas, and tossed one across the room. The cat flew from the table and pounced on the ball.

The jingly toy would keep her entertained. She stared down at Spencer's iPad. His designs were so good and so wonderfully eccentric. Why on earth did he have so much faith that she could come up with something at that level?

The doorbell rang and she glanced up at the clock hanging in her kitchen, her heart pounding against her rib cage. *He's here.*

*Calm down.* She gave her chest a pat. *You've spent most of your week with this man.*

True, but this wasn't pulling his car out of a ditch or racing around a crowded ice rink. This was . . . She glanced at her tree.

Was this a date?

*Deep breaths.* She gave herself a mental pep talk and adjusted her long ponytail before pulling her red sweater over her hips. She stood in front of the intercom and buzzed him up, then counted to five to slow her heart before opening the door.

Her breath hitched as Spencer, looking ever-so-handsome in his black wool coat and red cashmere scarf, climbed the wooden stairs, a brown bag and a tray of drinks in his hands, a huge red velvet bag slung over his shoulder. "Ho, ho, ho!"

"I didn't realize Santa had a son."

That got a giant laugh. "Definitely keeping this bag for Halloween next year."

"What is all this?" she asked, eyeing the drinks.

"Our Christmas cocktails."

"You didn't have to do that." She opened the door wide. "And I thought I owed you a drink."

"You helped me beat the mayor." He winked. "That's really all I cared about. You more than deserve it."

She waved for him to enter. "Well, come on in."

"I grabbed an assortment of Chinese food. I hope that's okay."

Her stomach grumbled at the delicious aroma seeping through the bag. More than all right. "I didn't know Ling Lings sold gingerbread ale," she joked, taking the tray.

"I had an 'in' with the sponsor of last night's cocktail tent. Plus, I told her I'd stop calling her Gwennie if she hooked me up."

"I'm sure she was very happy to help you out."

"And I put in your request for crushed graham crackers."

"Yes!" Charlie led the way into her small kitchen. She pulled out the drinks and the tiny plastic bag of graham crackers with a piece a paper inside.

*What's this?* She unfolded the paper.

*Drink this Jingle Juice—fabulous night guaranteed. XO, G.*

She grinned and folded it back up, setting it aside. Leave it to her friend to send something that would help calm her nerves.

"What's that?" Spencer asked as he took off his coat and pulled out the Chinese food containers.

"Oh, nothing." She took his things, hanging both up on her coatrack, and then grabbed two small bowls out of her cabinet. After filling one with water and dumping graham cracker crumbs in the second, she dipped a glass rim into the water, then the coating. "Apparently, my best friend is now a fortune-teller."

He spooned some chicken onto a plate. "So, we're missing the Seven-Swans-a-Swimming tonight."

That they were, and she was totally fine with it. "I think we're still on Santa's good list. Some of the Elfcapades are geared for children, including tonight's." She planned on attending tomorrow night's Pizza & Pop Shop tree lighting only because it was her favorite, and the Pajama Rama that, up until last week, was a snooty ball she'd hoped to skip.

"Gotcha. I really love the whole Elfcapades concept. Last night was a total blast."

"Well, maybe you can come back next year." She added the cocktail to her graham- crusted glass, throwing in some smack talk. "But I'd completely understand if you're afraid that someone might upset your reign and force you to give back her golden goose."

That got a hearty chuckle. "That sounds like a challenge."

It took them a few minutes to fix their plates—happily, he'd purchased sesame chicken, broccoli in garlic sauce, a selection of egg rolls, and crab Rangoon. "We can relax in front of the television." She led the way out to the living room.

"Wow." Spencer said, pausing in the entryway. "That tree is . . ."

"It really is something." She set down her plate and took a seat, taking a sip of the toasted almond cocktail, the liquor making a delightful rush to her head. *Jingle juice, indeed.*

"Oh, I've got the decorations in my sister's minivan. After dinner, I can bring them up." Spencer took a seat next to her and was immediately greeted by a curious Jingles, who jumped onto his lap, rubbing her tiny head against Spencer's black sweater. "I take it this is the infamous Jingles."

"That's my sweetie, and I'm sorry." She reached over and picked up her cat. "She loves company. Jingle Bells, why don't you check out the tree? I know you want to go investigate." She set her down on the carpet and gave her a soft nudge.

"So, talk to me." He opened the bag of crab Rangoon and offered her one. "What happens at a Charlie Dobbs's tree-trimming party?"

It'd been five years since the last time she'd trimmed a tree with anyone who didn't have four paws. It was nice to have someone to participate in what had been one of her favorite Christmas pastimes. "My mom and I would start with takeout. Just like this really, but usually Pop's calzones."

"Love it. What else?"

"Well, then we'd put in *It's a Wonderful Life* and begin decorating. We usually started by stringing popcorn." She paused, her voice soft. "We always had such a good time."

"Had? That sounds like a wonderful tradition. Why did you stop?"

"She died five years ago from brain cancer."

"Oh wow. I'm so sorry. I didn't know."

"Thank you." Her throat grew thick.

"Your tradition with her sounds like it was really special. I'm sure you have all kinds of memories."

"I do. It really was super fun." She turned toward him, bringing her leg under her and getting comfy. She wanted to lighten the conversation and enjoy this rare opportunity to reminisce with someone. "My dad would always join in too. Usually to help string the lights, but we would always put him on popcorn duty."

"Popcorn duty." He took a bite of his chicken. "I like it."

She grinned. "Some of my favorite times with my parents have been around this holiday. I offered to keep the tree-trimming tradition going, but my dad's never been up for it. He doesn't even put up a tree anymore." She sighed. "Even me . . . I love picking out my tree, but trimming it . . ." her voice trailed for a couple of seconds, and she picked it back up before her eyes started to flood. "Some years feel like I'm just going through the motions."

He tapped her knee. "Well, this tree-trimming party is going to be like no other. You'll be reminiscing about it for years."

"Oh, really? That sounds intriguing." Her gaze landed on the Santa sack Spencer had set down by the door. "And speaking of trees, if there aren't Christmas decorations in there, what's inside?" Her eyes widened. "Is it Brookie? If so, I can't believe you've left her stuffed in there this long."

"You can relax. Brooklyn's enjoying a night in, perched on a toasty spot on the mantel above my parents' fireplace." He waggled his eyebrows. "You're dying to see what's inside, aren't you?"

"I wouldn't say dying." She stood and took their finished plates to the kitchen. Stopping in the archway, she looked over her shoulder to see Spencer reach for one of Jingles's toy bells and dangle it in front of the cat. Jingles's front paws flew in the air.

She grinned and set the plates in the sink. No. If there was ever a time that she was enjoying every single breath, it was right now.

She grabbed her phone off the counter and took a picture of the two playing with the jingle bells in front of the tree. Maybe she could text it to Spencer later as proof he could do Christmas in Brooks Bend.

Her insides warmed at the thought of him next Christmas, tossing bells across the floor for Jingles to pounce on. *Slow down, girl.* Talk about putting the sleigh in front of the reindeer.

"Would you like something else to drink?" she called

out, moving back into her kitchen and opening the refrigerator. She didn't have an ale, but maybe he'd like some eggnog.

"I'm good, thanks."

"I'm just going to rinse off the dishes real quick." Minutes later, she returned to the living room, her mouth flying open. On her carpet, Spencer had laid out the most beautiful flannel fabric in Christmas colors: red, green, silver, gold, and shimmering light blue. "What's all this?"

"I told you I was going to help with your design. I thought some fabric choices were in order."

She dropped to her knees beside him and ran her hand over the velvety soft flannel. This wasn't material that could be picked up at any retail fabric store. "Where did you get this?"

"I took a trip into the city." He nodded, petting Jingles, who'd now made a new friend and was rubbing her head against Spencer's arm. "Kristina wanted the kids to see the Rockefeller tree. We got them iced hot chocolate. You should have seen their faces light up."

"For the tree or the iced hot chocolate?"

He laughed. "Both. After that, we hit up the Garment District. My friend, Donovan, hooked me up with all this material."

"Well, thank you for this." She nodded toward her notepad and let out a deep sigh. *I guess it's time to fess up.* "Okay, I did do my homework and wrote down every word that reminded me of Christmas. I'm not sure it helped."

"It will. We can brainstorm while we decorate. So where's the popcorn?" He stood and looked around. "Do you need me to make it?"

"Oh no." She rolled up. "I abandoned that tradition when my tree grew by five feet."

"You sure? I'm all in."

That declaration warmed her inside as a vision of Spencer and her on the couch stringing popcorn, laughing the entire time. "It's okay. Maybe next year."

He gave her a blank look, placing a hand on her neck.

"Um, I mean, maybe the next time you're in Brooks Bend for the holidays and have some free time."

His stare softened into a smile. "I'd like that." He pointed to the front door. "I'll go grab those ornaments, and we can get started."

While Spencer retrieved the boxes, she searched her DVR for her recording of *It's a Wonderful Life*.

Setting the remote down, she admired all the fabric. What a sweet surprise. He was really doing everything in his power to help. She needed to come through with at least one idea.

Jingles waltzed over, stepped onto one of the pieces, and flashed her belly. "Oh, no, you don't. I doubt Spencer's customers want to wear gray cat hair next Christmas."

It took Spencer a few short minutes to bring the boxes in, and they got started unpacking the contents. Charlie reached for four bags of silver tinsel.

"My mom bought the tinsel for you today," Spencer said, pulling out a tray of red and gold ornament balls.

"That was awfully nice of her."

"She said a Christmas tree not tinseled is merely a decorated tree, whatever that means." He set aside the ornament balls, digging deeper into the box. "Oh wow. I can't believe she kept this all these years." Spencer pulled out a tiny Christmas sweater ornament. "I made this in third grade. Check it out."

"Wow." She eyed the red sweater with a tree outlined in green pipe cleaner strips and a bright orange pom-pom for the treetop. "It's . . ."

"Tacky. I know."

"Tacky Christmas sweaters are all the rage." She handed it back to him. "Look at third-grade you being a trendsetter."

"Ha, hardly." He reached in the box and pulled out a box of glittery red ornament balls. "Want to know a Christmas tradition that always looks like fun, but I've never felt comfortable in my own skin to bring myself to do?"

There was something the confident Spencer Carmichael was afraid to do? She had to hear this. "What's that?" She pulled out the lights, beginning to untangle the cord. "Standing in line outside an electronics store at midnight for Black Friday."

"No. Never had that desire." He chuckled, running his thumb over his homemade ornament. "Wear a tacky

Christmas sweater to a party."

She stopped untangling, glancing over. "You had one on the other day. The snowman." That sounded insulting. "I mean . . . it was cute."

"That was my dad's, and I had on my coat."

"I think it would still qualify as tacky."

"Well, okay, maybe, but it wasn't to a party with intent." He held up his ornament. "Warwick's throws a tacky Christmas sweater party every year for its corporate employees, but I always stop in, in my suit and tie."

"Why not throw on a sweater?" She set the first strand of lights to the side and began working on the other. "Surely Warwick's must carry Christmas ones." With his skills, he could probably create one in an hour.

He shrugged his shoulders. "I guess I'm just more comfortable in a suit and tie most days."

"Well, maybe you should give it a try next year, or throw a small one of your own."

"Maybe."

Oh, right. The Man with the Bag, who blew out of town before Christmas. "Tell you what. You throw the tackiest Christmas sweater party next year, and I'll be there. I'll be sure to be wear—"

His face fell.

*Oh, geez.* She reached for her drink. Inviting herself to his apartment a whole year from now probably wasn't the best idea. Picking up the lights, she stood. "You ready to start stringing?"

"As long as I don't have to light them."

They began stringing the lights, working their way around the tree as *It's a*

*Wonderful Life* continued to play. Working in unison, they found an easy rhythm, and in no time, they reached a height where Charlie could go forth alone. "I think I've got this if you want to start hanging the ornaments."

"Sure thing." Spencer moved to the coffee table and grabbed a red, glittery ball. He hung it up, stepped back and crossed his arms for a few seconds before pulling the ornament off the branch and sliding it on to another, stepping back again.

"Um . . . Spencer. The tree needs to be decorated before Christmas."

His laugh filled her apartment. "It will . . . it'll look spectacular when I'm done." He winked. "When we're done," he corrected. He hung a few more ornaments that way before finally saying, "So, Charlie Dobbs, tell me about your greatest weakness."

"What?" She finished hanging the last strand and stood.

Spencer hung another glittery red ball, took three steps back, and folded his arms. "They're going to ask that question in your interview. It's almost a guarantee."

"Hmm." She watched him slide another ornament hanger into a red ball and place it on the tree, repeating his process.

She had to admit, the ornament balls were perfectly placed around the tree. "Okay, here's an answer." She picked up a silver glass ball and took it over to the tree, sliding it on a branch.

"Sometimes, I'm so focused on the task at hand that I tend to not step back to see the big picture." She took three steps back to where he stood, folded her arms, waited a beat, and then removed the silver glass ball. She slid it on a better branch that had no ornaments near it. "I don't see that I've missed a branch."

"Well done." He unfolded his arms. "Although you should probably leave Christmas trees out of your answer."

"Probably."

Spencer asked another question and then another as she helped him perfectly position all the glass balls around the tree.

"Thank you for this. I've been rehearsing by myself, but it really helps to have someone to practice answering potential questions."

"You're welcome." He appeared from the back of the tree. "You're going to do great."

She smiled, grabbing a large amount of the silver tinsel his mom had bought for her and giving him a handful. "So, the technique for tinseling a tree is very simple." She threw her fistful.

He groaned but nevertheless tossed the tinsel. "Like this?"

She nodded triumphantly, flicking more tinsel onto the tree. "Just like that."

She hadn't thought it would be possible to trim a tree and not feel the loss of her mother, but tonight was proving she could participate in a time-honored family tradition in a new way.

And it could start by filling the room with festive holiday cheer. She grabbed her remote and switched the movie to some Christmas music, cranking it up.

"Now, you're talking." Spencer flung more tinsel onto the tree. He went to adjust the amount that landed, and she playfully swatted his hand away.

"It's perfect."

He smiled and continued to throw it on, shaking his hips and spinning around.

They rocked their way around the tree, dancing and laughing. Spencer took several opportunities to show off his moves when the song "The Man with the Bag" came on with a smooth moonwalk across her hardwood floor, followed by grabbing her hand and twirling her around. Finally, he climbed her step stool to place the star on top.

Her heart filled with all kinds of emotion she wasn't ready to name. Seeing Spencer finish decorating this tree that he'd handpicked and cut down for her was everything. Unlike the picture she took of him and Jingles, she wouldn't need physical proof to remember this moment.

There was only one thing left to do. She picked up the

cord to the lights. "Would you like to do the honors?"

He grinned and hopped off the step stool, moving it aside. "I'm good."

She plugged in the white Christmas lights and maneuvered over to her living room lamp, dimming it.

"Oh, wow, Charlie. It's stunning."

It really was that and more. "Thank you for the tree and the ornaments." Her eyes started to water as her gaze met his. "It's been a long time since I've done this," she whispered, not entirely sure she was only talking about trimming a Christmas tree.

He smiled down at her. "You have tinsel in your hair." He reached over and pulled out a silvery string, his finger lingering on her cheek. "You're so beautiful," he said, his mouth inching closer to hers.

She lifted her chin, and her lips parted as she closed her eyes, wanting to show this man all that she was feeling in this moment—all that she was feeling for him.

"Uh, I should probably get going."

Her eyelids flew open. Spencer had stepped back. Disappointment rushed through her. Had she misread things? Her cheeks began to flame. "Yeah, of course."

"It's getting late. You've got a big day tomorrow, and I want to get some things done before I help your dad paint the office. Plus, my sister needs me to help her wrap presents after the kids go to bed. They should be asleep by now."

While she was thrilled he was spending some holiday

time with his sister, he really didn't need to go on ticking off more reasons why this night was over. The message had been received.

She maneuvered away from the tree and turned up the lamplight. "Thank you so much for dinner, and please thank your mom for letting me borrow these decorations. I had a really nice time tonight."

"Me too, Charlie." He went over and grabbed his coat and scarf off the hook. "I'll see you tomorrow." His blue eyes locked on hers. "Good luck with your interview. I know you'll ace it."

"Thank you." She locked the door behind him and began to clean up. It really had been a spectacular evening of laughing and dancing around the tree. Isn't that what Christmas should be about?

The near-kiss shouldn't ruin it. They had both gotten caught up in a sweet moment. That was all.

She grabbed his red ideating ball and gave it a bounce on her kitchen table. It was probably for the better that he'd stepped away. Who needed that kind of complication?

She didn't.

She set the ball down and turned to see Jingles sprawled out again on the red fabric, holding one of her toy jingle bell balls between her paws.

She grabbed her phone, unable to resist taking a photo, then grinned down at the one before it of Spencer playing with Jingles.

*Oh my God! That's it.* The perfect design for Christmas pajamas. She nudged awake a miffed Jingles. "Jingles, you're a genius."

She raced into her bedroom and grabbed her glue gun and fabric sheers. Minutes later, she cut through the red fabric, gluing her cat's toy jingle bells onto the side.

Maybe she'd misread the moment, and maybe nothing would ever develop between them, but Spencer had given her something special tonight—the ability to enjoy a Christmas tradition she'd thought she'd lost forever.

It was time to do something for him. After all, Christmas was filled with moments that made you dance and those that made you laugh. Why not wear them?

# Chapter Fifteen

"WHO WANTS A Frosty the Snowman pancake?" Spencer pushed in chocolate chips for the eyes and nose and then gingerly wrapped a bacon strip around the two pancakes for Madeline's snowman, doing the same, but also making tiny, round eyeglasses out of black licorice for Ben's. He stepped back and admired the pancakes, perfectly covered in shimmering whipped cream.

He reached for the coffeepot and filled his cup, picking up his sketch pad with his other hand. On his drive home from his incredible night with Charlie, a fabulous idea had hit him.

He took his silver pencil now, running long thin strokes along the bottoms of his latest design.

"Thank you, Uncle Spencer," the children said in unison, taking their seats at the two-foot-tall kids' table his mother had set up for them in front of the bay window.

"You're most welcome." He set his sketch down and sipped his coffee, taking a moment to enjoy Ben and Madeline tearing apart in seconds what had taken him an hour to make.

He couldn't help but chuckle to himself. Must be how Mom felt all those Christmases growing up when his sister and he would fly down the stairs, plop under the tree, and rip through the presents she'd no doubt spent hours meticulously wrapping to perfection.

Charlie's assembly-line process probably would have been the better approach when it came to breakfast pancakes smothered in whipped cream.

His insides grew warm, and he picked up her clipboard, scanning her to-do list. They both agreed he'd help her dad paint the auto shop's office later today. Maybe there was something else on her list he could get done.

"They really are having fun with their favorite uncle," Kristina said as she joined them in the kitchen and pulled out a stool, hopping on.

"Favorite?" He set the clipboard aside, reaching for the coffeepot and pouring a cup for his sister. "Oh, right. Pete has two brothers." He lowered his voice. "Are you feeling better about things?"

"I wouldn't say better. I feel a little empty. I'm sure it will be different next year."

He gave his sister a supportive smile. "Well, speaking of next year, maybe you all could come visit me for Christmas." He took a sip of his coffee.

"I don't think we want to go to the Bahamas."

"I won't be there."

"You won't?"

He shook his head.

Kristina bounced up. "Well then, I'd love it. The kids had so much fun yesterday seeing the Rockefeller tree."

"That might be a problem." He leaned against the sink.

"What do you mean?"

He set his coffee cup on the counter and crossed his arms. It was time to let his family in on his big news. Maybe saying it out loud would stir up some excitement inside him. "I'm moving to Italy."

"What?" Kristina's palms slammed down on the kitchen island. "Why? When?"

"I got a job offer. A big one. It's been in the works for a few months, but the official word came a couple of days ago. I leave for Milan after the New Year."

"Milan? Oh my God, Spencer. That's terrific." She came around the island and gave him a big hug. "Kids, your uncle is moving to Italy."

That got thirty seconds of interest, tops, before his niece and nephew went back to enjoying their pancakes.

"Italy. Wow." His sister seemed to not be able to get over that news. "Do you even know Italian?"

"*Buon giorno*," he offered, hand in the air. "That's about it."

She snapped her fingers. "I think I know what I'm getting you for Christmas. I can't believe it. My little brother's leaving New York City." Her eyes suddenly went wide. "Wait. What about your Christmas pajamas? The Man with the Italian Bag doesn't sound the same."

It really didn't. "I'll be working with Warwick's as their first creative director-in-residence. I'll have my own clothing line of eco-friendly designs—tops, pants, skirts, you name it. I'll be alongside some of the best designers in the business. I hope that I'll continue to design the S.C. holiday pajamas too."

"It does sound like an incredible opportunity. Do Mom and Dad know?"

"Not yet. I'll get around to telling them today." He nodded to the kids. "Or they will."

He rinsed out his coffee, setting the mug in the sink. He should be showing off his dance moves and moonwalking along his parents' aluminum floor, but instead, he picked up Charlie's clipboard.

"It really is all I ever wanted." His voice trailed off as he gazed over Charlie's task to cut down a Christmas tree. "It will take my career to an entirely different level," he said, reaching for a nearby pen. He uncapped it and checked that item off her list, as well as picking up Lillian Lathrop's part and the office paint.

"But . . ."

He looked up. "But what?"

"Do I hear some hesitation?"

"I don't know." He set the clipboard down, threading his fingers and cracking his knuckles. "Timing, maybe."

"Timing," she repeated, leaning her elbows on the island,

her expression all kinds of curious. "Does a pretty blonde who knows her way around a V8 engine have something to do with your hesitation?"

Was it that obvious? "Maybe. If I knew what one was," he joked, but admitted, "I really like her, Kristina."

"No! I couldn't tell," she teased. "At all."

"She's just so cool and easy to talk to. I have fun around her, and it's weird."

"Why would it be weird?" His sister pushed off the counter and reached for a strip of bacon, taking a bite.

"We just met. I don't know all that much about her except that she fixes cars for a living but is looking to do something different; has a really funny sense of humor, but embarrasses easily, and she loves Christmas—totally into this holiday. Maybe just as much as Mom."

Kristina grabbed another piece of bacon. "Sounds like you're on your way to getting to know her. I wouldn't worry too much about it happening quickly. When I met Pete, we started dating exclusively two weeks later."

"Yeah, but that's different. You were doing your residencies together. Charlie and I probably wouldn't have even met if she hadn't pulled me out of a ditch."

"I still say she should have left you there."

He grinned at his sister's teasing, but silently, he was grateful that he hadn't had the good sense to stay off The Vine that night.

"You know, she told me that she's interviewing for a job

in New York City. How ironic is that? I finally meet a woman I'd like to get to know better, and I'm going to be an ocean away from her."

"Timing," his sister said, making herself a pancake.

"I think I'm going to head up to my room, spend some time at my old art desk for old times' sake."

"Good luck," his sister called out as he headed with his sketch pad and pencils out of the kitchen, stopping at his parents' Christmas tree and grabbing a fistful of tinsel.

Three hours later, he stepped back from his completed design of a silhouette in shimmering silver pajamas with red and silver tinsel fringe along the sides and bottom hem.

The design was fresh, fun, and festive. One of his best yet.

He spun around and fist pumped the air, fueled by exhilaration and relief.

"I'm back!"

# Chapter Sixteen

"THANK YOU, CHARLIE. It was so great to meet you."

"It was wonderful to meet you too." Charlie shook David Barlow's hand. "I thoroughly enjoyed our conversation and learning more about your company and the position. I really can see myself thriving here."

Charlie made her way out of the building and walked the four blocks to 42nd Street, her pulse racing as she pulled her phone out of her purse and checked the time. The interview had been a solid three hours.

The practice questions Spencer had asked her last night had been spot-on. She'd been able to answer everything thrown at her with confidence, explain her background and why she was interested in joining Barlow Automotive Designs. Her prepared questions had led to a wonderful conversation that helped her understand the job better and the people on the team.

She placed a hand over the butterflies in her stomach. *Thank you all for standing down. Well done.*

She scrolled through her phone contacts for Gwen's number. Her friend picked up immediately.

"Tell me everything."

"I think it went well." Charlie crossed another street, picking up her step with all the other businessmen and women, probably on their lunch breaks. "They asked a number of questions and gave me a tour. They even have a showroom displaying all of their innovations." Her confidence built with every step. "You know, I think I could really see myself here. They told me they're looking to make a decision by the end of the week."

"That soon?"

"I know, right? Apparently, they want someone to hit the ground running in the new year." They continued to catch up as Charlie made her way toward Grand Central Station. "You know if I move here, I'm going to demand that you visit me pretty much every other weekend."

"Deal. Oh, and by the way, did you see the weather report for tonight?"

Of course she did, given what she currently did for a living. And yes, she could admit that she was a little curious to see if it would be snowing during the Pizza & Pop Shop tree lighting—that backdrop could be super romantic. She shook her head. "Even if it snows, I don't think Spencer and I are going to happen."

"But you want it to! That's progress."

"Okay, I like him, you win." Charlie stopped in front of a beautiful Christmas window display that looked like a winter wonderland with skaters skating on an outdoor pond.

Glancing up, she caught the iconic blue Warwick's sign.

Her breath hitched. *This is where Spencer works.* "Hey, Gwen. I've got to run. Are you doing anything tomorrow night?"

"Not really. I planned to hang out in the boutique and tackle some inventory. Why?"

"Mind helping me with my Jingle Jammies design? I could really use your eye and expertise."

"Ooh, your design has a name."

She smiled into the phone. It *was* her design—well, concept, anyway—and it was a fun one. "I'll tell you all about it when I see you." She ended the call and headed into Warwick's, passing through the makeup and handbag displays to the clothing area. She finally found sleepwear on the second floor and began to browse the different pajama sets.

"If you're looking for S.C. pajamas, unfortunately, we aren't carrying any this year, but next year's are going to be spectacular."

Charlie spun around to see a striking woman bundled up in a pink wool coat. Her wavy black hair fell well past her shoulders. *How does she know they'll be spectacular?* Charlie hadn't even told Spencer her idea. "I was just hoping maybe there would be some from last year, but that's okay."

"You're a friend of Spencer's?" the woman asked, her white smile brightening.

"Um . . ." *What are we?* Their nearly kissing last night had caused him to sprint out of her apartment at flying reindeer speed, so there still wasn't a clear way to define whatever was going on between them. "I'm from his hometown."

The women's eyes went wide. "You're from Brooks Bend."

"I am." Charlie nodded. It wasn't nearly as exciting as this stranger seemed to think—and who was this woman, anyway? Whoever she was, she was sporting one huge rock of ice on her left hand. "I'm actually headed back to meet up with Spencer." She took a step to leave.

"Hey, would you mind taking something to him? I have his present and was going to wait until the new year to give it to him, but it'd be nice for him to have it for Christmas. It's just upstairs in my dad's office."

Charlie slipped her hands into her coat pockets. It was a little weird to go above the store level. Still, she was curious to get an insider's tour of where Spencer worked. "Sure. I'd be happy to."

"Thank you so much. Follow me." The woman extended a hand at the elevator. "I'm Mandy Warwick Adler, by the way."

"Oh." Charlie's shook the woman's hand. "Of Warwick's?"

"Yes. My great-grandfather opened the department store in 1937. My father is the current CEO." She sighed. "Department stores are a dying breed, but my dad and his team are always working their magic to reinvent Warwick's.

Spencer's a big part of our brand." She winked. "He's also like a big brother to me."

Charlie smiled at that admission. It more than likely was the reason he'd been so devastated over the failed pajamas. He'd let his Warwick's family down. "It's nice to meet you. I'm Charlie Dobbs."

"What do you do in the city, Charlie?"

She caught her reflection in the elevator. That question was no doubt based on her long coat, suit, and high boots. "I'm actually interviewing. Just came from one."

"That's terrific. Good luck. There's no better place in the world to work than New York City." Mandy escorted Charlie up to the tenth floor. "If you don't mind waiting for a second in Spencer's office, I'll go grab the gift from my dad's assistant." She started to walk down the hallway, but turned. "Charlie, what pajama size are you?"

"Um . . ." Charlie blinked. "Medium."

"Great. I'll be right back. Make yourself comfortable." Mandy disappeared down the hall.

She stepped into the corner office. *Make myself comfortable. This wasn't weird at all.* Her high boots clicking on the shiny marble floor as she took in a beautiful mahogany desk and black leather chairs. Off to the side was a more contemporary looking drawing desk and a long mahogany table along the window.

Her pulse quickened as she walked over to the giant sketch pad on the drawing desk. It felt a little wrong to be walking so casually in Spencer's ordinary world without him here. Her gaze rested on a sketch of a woman's silhouette wearing a lacy, short sleeve top with the words *Eco-Friendly Couture by Accettare* along the bottom.

On his desk, she spotted a framed photo of a younger Spencer in a red graduate gown and cords with his parents and sister. Another framed picture of Spencer—on a boardwalk with Ben and Madeline enjoying ice cream cones, the blue ocean in the background—sat next to it.

Her heart melted as she picked up the second photo. He really did prefer the scorching hot sun over cold, blowing snow.

"They are cuties, aren't they?"

"Yes, definitely." She set down the photo. "They're so much bigger now."

"I'd love to meet them someday." Mandy smiled, set a red gift bag down on Spencer's desk, and handed Charlie a set of pale-blue pajamas decorated with bells and wings. "I found a pair of Spencer's first S.C. design for us in the inventory closet."

Charlie's breath hitched as she held the soft jammies. Kristina had said during the Geese-a-Laying Contest that his first design had been inspired by *It's a Wonderful Life*. "Thank you. Should I pay for them downstairs?"

Mandy waved a dismissive hand. "You're doing me a big favor taking Spencer his present." She rummaged through the red gift bag. "I just want to make sure one of the gifts is the right one." She chuckled. "I love my dad's assistant, but sometimes she gets her pictures mixed up. My in-laws got a nice framed one last year of random employees in our warehouse playing beer pong."

She took out a small box, opened the lid, and pulled back tissue. "Phew. We just took this last week." She handed the frame to Charlie.

In the middle was Spencer in the black suit and red tie he'd worn the night she towed his car out of the snowbank, along with Mandy and a few other people she assumed had some relationship to Warwick's—all wearing tacky Christmas sweaters.

She couldn't help but chuckle. "I'm sorry. I don't mean to laugh. It's just that Spencer mentioned that he's yet to wear a tacky Christmas sweater to your party."

Mandy nodded. "Oh, yes. Our guy has a hard time embracing Christmas, silly traditions and all."

The way she said *our guy* with that wide, assuming grin made Charlie's cheeks warm. "Well, from what I've seen, I think he's having a good time finding his inner Christmas. So far, he's cut down a Christmas tree, successfully identified different holiday scents, including eggnog and fruitcake, while blindfolded, and taken home our town's coveted golden goose. And his Christmas cookie decorating skills are insane."

Mandy threw her hands in the air. "I *knew* a proper Christmas holiday, not on a beach, was all he needed. He's going to come back next year with a fabulous design." She narrowed her lashes. "I'm guessing you know about this year's."

"I did know," she said slowly. Though she could tell Mandy was someone she'd really like, it didn't seem appropriate to spill the beans that she was helping him. "He's going to come up with something fabulous. It'll be so . . ." Her thoughts went to the prototype fabric with glued bells, currently on top of her closet and away from Jingles's curiosity. "Festive and fun."

"Festive and fun," Mandy repeated. "I like it. I'm going to blow up my social media with nothing but love for his new design. It's the least I can do after last week."

Charlie's mouth flew open. "Are you the influencer whose pajamas caught on fire?"

"They were my husband's pair, and it was really only a little smoke." Mandy made a tiny motion with her fingers and snickered. "Tell you the truth, Charlie, between us girls, it was funny seeing my NFL boo squealing around our condo. Tye's got a lot of kids who love him, and they probably would've cracked up to see him carrying on like a scared little baby. Manly football player and all." She shook her head, still laughing. "Don't tell Spencer or my husband I said that."

Charlie crossed her lips and glanced down one last time at the photo.

An idea hit her. The perfect top for her jingle jammies.

"Hey, Mandy. Where downstairs would I find the tacky Christmas sweater collection?"

"Third floor. We've got a whole collection of holiday couture, including a tacky sweater line. We're talking *ugly*."

"Excellent." She grinned and picked up Spencer's gift bag and started to leave as yet another brilliant idea took shape. One that could help Spencer while no doubt delighting all the kids attending the Pajama Rama.

"Mandy, what are you and your husband doing on Christmas Eve?"

# Chapter Seventeen

CHARLIE PULLED HER truck in and shoved it in park, smiling at the three Warwick's bags stuffed with tacky sweaters she'd hauled on the train back to Brooks Bend.

Maybe this crush she'd developed wasn't going anywhere, given Spencer's reaction last night, but it didn't matter. She wanted to help him get his career back on track. It was easy to see that his relationship with Warwick's ran deeper than a paycheck.

She hopped out and grabbed his gift bag from Mandy. Opening the door to the auto body shop, she called out, "Hey, guys, I'm ba—" The words died in her throat. Spencer stood facing the wall in a white T-shirt and brown overalls, spreading light-blue paint.

His right arm was covered in it.

He turned around and his eyes went wide, the roller brush suspended in air. "Wow. You look amaz—"

"You're dripping everywhere!" She set the gift bag on the office desk and rushed over, squatting down and picking up the tray. "Here."

"You look terrific," he said, holding the brush over the

tray and taking it from her.

Her heart sped up as she removed her coat and hung it on the coatrack outside the office. "Thank you. It took an hour or so not to feel like a total fish out of water."

"How'd your interview go?" he asked, rolling another layer onto the wall.

"Really well."

"Tell me all about it. Did they ask you the greatest weakness question?"

She took a few minutes to fill him in, which took a few minutes more because he had a million questions. It was nice to have someone to share in her excitement.

More than nice.

"I should know in a few days." She picked up the gift bag. "I stopped at your department store. This is for you."

He stopped painting and glanced over his shoulder. "You went to Warwick's?"

"Yeah, I had some time to kill before getting back on the train and walked by it." She flashed a smile. "Naturally, I had to go in."

He dipped his paint roller into the tray, rolling it back and forth. "There are a lot of good sales this time of year, but you didn't have to get me anything."

"Oh, I didn't. It's from Mandy."

That declaration got a big eyebrow lift. "Mandy Warwick Adler?"

"Uh-huh. We bumped into each other on the floor and

got to talking. Once she realized I was from Brooks Bend and knew you, she asked me if I could bring you this." Charlie left out the part of being in his office. "I didn't tell her that I was helping you with your pajamas design."

"Wouldn't care if you did." He winked, and darned if it wasn't the cutest. "Although, I'd have some explaining to do."

She watched as he rolled the roller brush along the wall, the overalls accentuating his broad shoulders. *Spencer Carmichael in auto mechanic grubs.* Who would have thought? How ironic that they'd traded professional attire. "Did my dad lend you those overalls?"

"Yeah." He gave a suspender a flick with his free hand. "I can see why you like to wear these so much."

"*Those* aren't mine. But yes, they're very comfy." She laughed and scanned the garage. "By the way, where is my dad?"

"You're never going to believe it."

"Try me." She opened the small closet, searching for an extra pair of overalls she could throw on to help. From the one wall that was half-done, it was clear that, left alone, Spencer was using his "let me examine the paint and how the light reflects on it while drying" process.

"He's up at The Vine."

"Oh no. Is everything okay?" she asked, pulling out the infamous red overalls she'd been wearing when Evan kicked her out of the ribbon-cutting photo. She could wear them with a long black knit sweater she'd also stuffed in the closet and an extra pair of work boots.

"He's chopping down a Christmas tree with Dee Dee. She picked him up about an hour ago."

"What?" She popped her head out of the closet, her jaw way open. "For real?"

"Yep. They left here like two giggling teenagers on a mission. I told them they needed to chop down their tree before dark."

"Wow," was really all she could say at first. Then she cocked her head. "How did the topic of cutting down a Christmas tree even come about?"

He brought a step stool over, climbed up, and ran a small paintbrush along the top of the wall. "Well, we got to talking about things while I was mixing colors."

"Why were you mixing the paint?" She set the overalls down and pulled open the desk drawer, reaching for a hair tie she always kept in there. "I selected a certain color blue."

"Not important to the story."

She pulled her hair into a long ponytail, suspecting the blue on the wall was an S.C. original, not the paint store. "Okay, go on."

"I was telling him about the great time I had picking out your tree and how fun it was to trim it with you, and before I knew it, he asked me if I wouldn't mind painting the rest alone."

"Unbelievable." Charlie stood speechless.

"Yeah. I'm surprised he trusted me with three unpainted walls."

"Well. No, I just can't believe he's finally getting a tree." *And with Dee Dee.* Was her dad taking a step forward with the diner owner?

Spencer stopped painting, glancing down. "I hope I didn't overstep."

She shook her head. "No. I think it's great that he's ready to have a Christmas tree again." She hopped off the desk. "Please tell me you didn't encourage him to chop down anything over five feet. He has a bad back."

"There was no encouragement to go up on desired tree length."

"Great." She dashed off to change, taking her phone with her. Alone in the restroom, she leaned against the door.

Her heart sped up. The way his eyes had widened when he saw her come in and his genuine interest in hearing about her interview had to mean something. That, or the fact he looked insanely hot in overalls, was doing a number on her.

Maybe she'd misread him bolting from her apartment last night. She swiped open her phone and touched the weather app icon.

*Please snow tonight. Please snow.*

Doing a celebratory jig at the snowflake icon crossing her screen, she changed and headed back into the office, grabbing a paint roller. With her fast strokes and cheerleading to pick up the pace, they finished in a little more than an hour.

"I think I have a pajama idea," she confessed, running her brush along the trim.

"What is it?" He moved his step stool next to hers and went over an area with his paintbrush that she'd missed.

"If it's okay, I'd like to have a couple of days to flesh it out a little more before I share. Gwen's going to come over and help. Maybe you could stop by the night after next. See what you think. Or we could meet up at Dee Dee's," she added, in case he'd prefer somewhere that wasn't her apartment.

"Your place would be fine. Probably more room to spread everything out."

"Yeah, definitely." She turned to the wall, frowning. He didn't tack on "it's a date" like he did at the ice rink.

They finished the trim and came down from their step stools, took three steps back, and folded their arms. She glanced up at him. "You know the original blue would have been just fine."

"But mixing in the eggshell white will make the room pop once it's dry. Trust me."

"I bet my dad will sell the garage for double the value now."

He laughed. "Maybe he will."

She picked up her phone off the desk to check the time. "Oh my God. Spencer, the Pizza & Pop Shop tree lighting starts in thirty minutes. We're going to miss it."

"Oh, elf, no. Not happening. I need that Christmas tree

pizza in my belly. I'm not missing out on that."

Charlie glanced out the garage window into the pitch-black night. "By the time we go home and change, they'll probably have run out. I'm so sorry. You're supposed to light the tree too."

"I am?" he asked, scratching some paint he'd gotten on his thumb.

"They didn't tell you?" From his puzzled expression, Mr. Skillman forgot to mention that when Spencer won the Geese-a-Laying Contest. "This year's winner of the golden goose is supposed to do the honors."

"They don't want me to light it unless a firetruck is nearby," he joked. "But on the other hand, if Mayor Drip gets the microphone, we'll be out there all night. Let's go."

"We can't go looking like this! I'm covered in paint." That much was true. She'd managed to get specks all over her overalls, in her hair, and probably on her face. "I need to at least go wash my face and change my clothes."

He reached for the brush and streaked his chin and his chest. "Now I'm covered too. Let's go."

She bit her lip. People were bound to stare and whisper when they showed up disheveled in overalls and blue paint, but it was nice that he now had a sense of humor when it came to lighting up a Christmas tree. It would be a shame if he missed this moment. "You're crazy if you don't think people are going to talk."

"Let 'em. I'm not embarrassed to show off a hard day's

work." He handed over her coat before sliding into his. "And I know you aren't."

"All right then." She took her coat. "Let's go get our Christmas tree pizza."

SPENCER TOOK AN enormous bite of the iconic Brooks Bend tree slice, his eyes rolling back as his taste buds reacted to the tomato sauce and special seasoning. "Man, New York City pizza is supposed to be the best, but this . . . this is everything."

"It is, isn't it?" Charlie took a bite, wiping her lips with a napkin as Gwen came up, showing off her red hat.

He stood back, flexing his legs, watching the two catch up. Today had been a great day. Inspired by their time together around her tree, he'd spent the entire morning, designing a set of pajamas with red and silver tinsel fringe on the top and bottom.

His backup pajamas that he was growing more confident he wasn't going to need. Charlie had this.

He inhaled the frosty air, taking in the crowd all around them. If someone would have told him that one of the best nights of his year would be spent chomping on pizza on a sidewalk in thirty-degree weather, dressed in overalls and covered in paint, he wouldn't have believed them.

A great night, but not the best.

Last night's tree decorating took that slot.

Well, up until the moment he'd full-blown chickened out. His lips had been inches from landing on Charlie's soft lips. In the moment, he couldn't do it.

He'd wanted to—oh, he'd definitely wanted to.

But then what? Was it fair to her to start something when he was moving clear across the Atlantic in days?

His gut reaction had been "no, it wasn't fair," and he'd stepped back. If her baby blues had met his, he knew he would have kissed her silly.

So instead, he'd bolted.

Dumbest thing he'd ever done.

"Do you want to head over to the tree?" Charlie asked as Gwen waved goodbye and took off down the street.

He blinked. "I think I'm going to grab another slice. My stomach is demanding an encore. How about you?"

"Would love one. Extra seasoning, please."

"You got it." He turned and smacked into the mayor and Jillian.

"Spencer. Charlie," Mayor Drip greeted them, zipping up his jacket to his chin. "Glad you both could make it on this nippy night."

"There's no other place I'd rather be." Spencer nodded toward the tree in the town's square. "I'm looking forward to lighting up that puppy."

Jillian, all bundled up in a black fur, her red scarf and gloves perfectly matching her pout, eyed Charlie up and down. "Surely, you could have cleaned up before you came? You live right up there." She pointed above the Pizza & Pop Shop as if Charlie needed a visual cue on how close she was to her apartment.

*What a piece of work.* Spencer glanced over at Charlie, who was now scratching the paint off her face with her finger, her radiant smile long gone.

Charlie had so much to celebrate tonight. She'd aced her interview that would inevitably create new, exciting opportunities and was on her way to showing him a design he knew he'd love. Jillian wasn't going to ruin it.

This petty patronizing ended now. He unzipped his jacket so Jillian could see he was wearing overalls and covered in paint too. "Charlie and I've been quite busy."

That admission got a questioning smirk from her ex.

But Spencer was ready to put both of these small-town snobs in their place. "We've been creating a masterpiece. Transforming the ordinary into the extraordinary by blending creative thought and skillful implementation. Charlie's task-orientated nature is an excellent balance to my creative ethos. The best partnership, if there ever was one." He grabbed her hand and gave it a swing. "If you'll excuse us, we're going to grab another slice before I light the tree." He winked, but couldn't resist one last dig. "Maybe next year, one of you will get that honor."

He escorted a dumbfounded Charlie away from Jillian and the mayor, shielding her from any lingering stares from the couple.

"Wow." Charlie shook her head. "That was . . . something."

"It needed to be said."

"You made painting the garage office quite the artistic expression."

"I did, didn't I? Well, I meant every word." He ordered two slices, making sure both had extra seasoning before handing one plate to her. "We make a good team. I feel my productivity meter going off the charts."

That brought her smile back and, man, was it gorgeous.

"Well, I'm learning that creativity and efficiency both need fuel, because I'm still ravenous." She hoisted her tree slice in the air toward him. "To Christmas pizza and lighting up trees."

"Hear! Hear! Hey, do I need to make a speech at this shindig?"

"You don't have an old relative who wrote a letter you could recite?"

"Nope."

"I get the feeling, unlike me, you're good at winging it."

"I've just had a little more practice." They ate their slices while strolling down Main Street, taking in the twinkling Christmas lights, along with the live, festive music that grew louder as they made their way to the square.

"So, Spencer, I meant to tell you earlier. I invited Mandy and Tye to the Pajama Rama."

"You met Tye too?"

"No. Just Mandy. I thought it could be nice to have her there for the pajama unveil, and I know the kids would be beside themselves to meet an honest-to-goodness NFL player."

He bit his lip. He no doubt had some explaining to do to Mandy and Roger since he hadn't yet shared the Pajama Rama with them or the fact that he'd elicited Charlie's help on the concept. "Yeah, that would be fun," he offered while working through his head what he was going to say tomorrow to his boss. Maybe he could take a trip to the city and talk to them in person. Give them an update.

"It was a bad idea, wasn't it? I can see it on your face. I'm so sorry."

"No, it's totally fine." His expression softened, and he placed a hand on her shoulder. "Really, everything is fine. They know I'm planning to have a design concept done by Christmas Eve. No biggie."

"It's totally fine," he repeated, more to convince himself than her. "And you're absolutely right. The kids are going to love Tye." They continued to walk in silence, finally reaching the end of the sidewalk. "So, you said when we were frosting cookies that this was one of your top five holiday traditions. Did our stroll live up to it?"

She smiled up at him, tipping her head. "It's almost perfect."

"Almost?" He cocked his head, curious and amused.

"What would make it perfect?"

"Maybe we can walk back in an hour," she said, humming as she headed in front of him across the street.

"What's happening in an hour?" He picked up his speed to catch up to her.

They joined his family, who'd gathered in the square's entrance, Charlie doing a round of cheery hellos to his parents and niece and nephew before spotting her dad and Dee Dee. "If you'll excuse me, I'm going to check on the teenagers."

"Go easy on them," he couldn't help but tease. "It's their first date."

She laughed and shook her head. "I'll meet you in front of the tree."

His heart began to accelerate. He hadn't asked her to stand with him at the ceremony, but she was the one person in town who knew how devastated he'd been last week at the disastrous light up of his pajama tree. It was a nice gesture.

Is this what it was like to have someone you had feelings for have your back?

"What on earth are you wearing, dear brother?"

He turned to see his sister holding two hot chocolates. She gave one to Madeline and the other to Ben.

"I was helping Fred and Charlie paint the auto shop's office."

"Did you get any on the wall? Blue is definitely your color." She touched the paint on his chin, lowering her voice.

"Have you told Charlie that you're leaving for Italy?"

"No. Not yet. I've been thinking. Maybe when I get back next year, if she's not seeing anyone, I could ask her out."

His sister grabbed onto his arm. "You can't go a whole year without telling her how you feel."

He let out a sigh. "I can't tell her how I feel and then leave for a whole year." It wouldn't be fair to her. That was, if she felt the same way about him. He glanced over at Charlie standing alone, looking cute in her long, messy ponytail with loose strands sliding down her face as she glanced up at the tree. "If you'll excuse me. I have a tree to light."

He made his way over just as Coach Skillman intercepted him with a microphone. "Spencer," he greeted him over the loud music. "Are you ready?"

"Yes." He locked eyes with Charlie, who gave him her thumbs-up. "I'm ready, Coach. Put me in."

"Can I have everyone's attention?" Coach Skillman welcomed the crowd. "We hope you have all enjoyed your Pizza & Pop Shop Christmas tree pizza. This year's proceeds benefit our recreation center on this eighth night of Elfcapades. Spencer, it's our pleasure to have you back in Brooks Bend, lighting up our tree for the seventy-eighth straight year."

"No pressure." Charlie held up her phone. "I promise I'm only taking a picture for you to have a keepsake and not to post on social media, but if something goes wrong, I've got you."

"Thanks for having my back."

She flashed him a smile. "You had mine last week at Evan's house. It's the least I can do."

"Spencer?" Coach Skillman handed over the microphone. "Would you like to say a few words?"

He stepped forward and took the microphone, turning to the crowd. "Hi, everyone. I'll keep this short so we can enjoy our pizza, this festive live music, and this magnificent tree." He shoved his free hand in his pocket. "You know, I wasn't planning on being here this year. I should have been toes up in the sand, but an ill-timed foot on the brake led me here to experience a Brooks Bend Christmas with all of you."

His gaze met Charlie's, her eyes full of encouraging warmth. "I can't say I was happy about it at first. You see, I kind of lost my Christmas way throughout the years, but I feel I'm now going in the right direction. I've enjoyed crawling for cocoa and taking home your beloved golden goose." He chuckled and turned in the direction of the mayor. "No hard feelings, Mr. Mayor."

Everyone turned to the mayor, who gave an awkward nod.

Spencer continued. "I'm having a blast, and finally, after thirty-four years, understand what Christmas is truly about. It's about family"—he waved to his—"and giving back to the community and making new friends." His gaze landed on Charlie. "And being with people who inspire you to let loose and have some fun, because that's what you should do this time of year.

"So, let's light this up. On the count of three. One . . . two . . . three." He plugged the cord into the outlet, the tree instantly illuminating in brightly colored bulbs. The crowd roared its applause and then joined the band in singing, "We Wish You a Merry Christmas."

He stepped back next to Charlie, lifting his head to take in all the colors on the magnificent tree. Maybe he'd failed with this year's pajama design, but tonight, he felt like a winner.

"Nice speech," she said, patting his shoulder.

"Thanks." He nodded up to the tree. "It's beautiful, but I think it's missing something."

"What's that?" she asked, scratching the paint on her cheek.

"Tinsel."

His gaze rested on the pretty smile that emerged; his pulse raced. *Don't be such a scaredy cat. Tell her how you feel.* He cleared his throat. "Charlie, I . . ." Just then, something cold hit his nose. By the look on Charlie's face, she felt it too.

"Spencer?" She turned to him. "Maybe we could go for that walk up Main Str—"

"I'm going to Italy," he blurted out. *Oh, for the love of God. Way to break that news.*

"Oh." A line formed between her brows.

He took a deep breath. "I'm moving there shortly after the new year. It's a year-long residency. An opportunity to work with a big fashion house in Milan and have my own eco-friendly line. I got word a few days ago that the residency is mine. It's all I've ever wanted." His voice cracked.

"Eco-friendly couture. Right." She stepped back, zipping her jacket up to her chin. "That's fantastic, Spencer. It sounds amazing. I'm happy for you."

"Thank you," was all he could manage to say, trying to read the expression in her eyes.

"Well, I should probably get going. We're supposed to get several inches of snow later, so I need to make sure I've got enough salt and sand in case someone needs a rescue. I'll see you in a couple of days." She started to walk away.

"I promise I won't be on The Vine tonight," he called out.

She whipped around, her ponytail flying as she pointed to him. "I'm going to hold you to that."

He watched as she stopped to say good-bye to her dad and Dee Dee before heading back up the street alone. He took a seat on a nearby bench and stared up at the brightly lit tree.

Italy was all he'd ever wanted.

His throat thickened as he looked down at the snowflakes that had begun to gather on his black wool coat and red scarf.

Until now.

# Chapter Eighteen

"**I**TALY? HOW ARE you two supposed to date from over there?"

Charlie brought in two glasses of Reisling and handed one to Gwen before taking a seat on her couch. She stretched out her legs, admiring the soft S.C. pajamas she'd put on an hour ago. She had to admit, they were the softest pj's she'd ever worn.

She'd been working on her own design for the second day straight, Gwen popping over during her lunch break and immediately after work both days to lend a hand. "That's a very good question."

And one she'd played out over and over. Her mom's master plan for snow to be falling the moment Charlie revealed her feelings would have never included the guy saying he was moving to Italy.

No, they were supposed to walk down Main Street in the snow along the twinkling lights. She'd invite him to come to her house later in the week for a home-cooked meal, and maybe, just maybe, before they parted, they'd kiss in the snow.

But that didn't happen. She glanced at the pad Thai containers she and Gwen had polished off.

She set her drink down on the end table and reached for the last decal to glue on her fourth jammies top. "He said he'll be there for a year working in some big fashion house. He seemed really excited." Reaching for her hot glue gun, she ran it along its edges. "I'm happy for him."

"Uh-huh." Gwen showed off the red bottoms she'd been working on, now with jingle bells perfectly glued down each side. "How do these look?"

Charlie clapped her hands. "Amazing."

Gwen gave them a shake, waking Jingles from her napping spot underneath the tree.

"It's perfect." She and her bestie had spent many hours over the last two days going to town with sheers, measuring tape and Charlie's mother's old sewing machine, transforming the fabric Spencer had given her into festive pajama tops and bottoms.

Gwen gave it another shake as Jingles jumped on the table.

"Stop teasing her." Charlie laughed, turning over the golden goose decal, pleased at the pattern she'd found on the internet. Gwen came over and plopped down on the couch, bringing her legs underneath her. "A year really isn't that long. Look at me and Luke."

"Yeah, but you both had been dating for two years before he went overseas." She picked up her mom's glue gun and ran it along the inside edges. "What if Spencer falls in love with the city and doesn't want to come back? Or,"—her chest tightened—"what if he falls in love?"

Gwen reached over and tugged Charlie's ponytail. "What if he's done that already?"

Charlie picked up the last white, long-sleeved top and placed the golden goose decal on the front, pressing into the fabric and holding it high in the air. "Brookie, you are going to be famous."

Gwen laughed. "I can't believe that golden goose is going to be a household name."

"Maybe. Spencer has to like the idea first." Just then, the doorbell rang in a serendipitous cue.

*He's here!* Her pulse quickened, and she jumped up. Charlie grabbed Gwen's hand, pulling her up too. "Go hide in my bedroom and put the bottoms on. When I call you, come out and jingle jam."

"Got it." Gwen cha-cha-cha'd into the bedroom and closed the door.

Charlie tugged the S.C. pajama top down and buzzed him up, opening the door. Her breath hitched as he climbed the stairs, his wool coat unbuttoned, revealing a blue suit and black tie. "Hi."

"Hey," he greeted her, his lips curving way up. "Look at you."

"Mandy gave them to me when I was at Warwick's," she admitted.

He beamed. "My first pair. Given your love for the movie, I hope you enjoy them."

"They are so comfortable. I now see what I've been missing all these years," she said, filling up her lungs with his spicy cologne. "You're all dressed up."

"I ended up going into the office today."

"Oh," she said, feeling slightly guilty for not sharing that she'd been in it too this week. "Everything okay?"

"Yeah, just felt inspired to get some things done." He winked. "But I've been looking forward to stopping over all day. Is this a good time?"

"Of course." She stepped aside as the butterflies lined up to deep dive into her stomach. "So, my design is inspired by your time here in Brooks Bend, since that was the charge you gave me the night of the Cookies and Cocoa Crawl."

He slipped out of his coat and followed her into the living room. "I'm intrigued."

She made her way to the coffee table. "I've created four tops representing our iconic traditions, but they also can be interpreted as tacky for those not from Brooks Bend."

His eyes danced as he took a seat. "Tacky Christmas sweater tops. I *love* it."

"You haven't even seen them yet." She laughed, her confidence growing as she picked up the first one on her coffee table and turned it over to reveal a Christmas tree pizza slice she'd decorated with snowflakes she'd cut out of the tacky Christmas sweaters she'd bought at Warwick's. "Here we've got Christmas pizza."

"Yes!" He chuckled.

"I knew you'd like this one, but it gets better." She held up the next shirt, displaying all kinds of cookies, a giant snowflake one in the middle. "Your snowflake cookie."

"My prize-winning snowflake cookie."

"Uh-huh." She set it on the coffee table. "Now, this next one I know you're going to love," she said teasingly, holding up a top with pointy elf shoes in the center.

And yep, he burst out laughing. "Does that one come in a large?"

"It does." She tossed it to him. "And last, and my favorite of the four icons that perfectly represent a Brooks Bend Christmas"—she picked up her favorite top and draped it in front of her, showing off the golden bird—"Brookie!"

"Wow. Wow. Wow. That is something."

"I mean, you are known for feathers, so why not show the whole bird?"

He grinned, taking in all her designs. "These are really fun, Charlie, and I love the tacky sweater concept for the top. Well done. What about the bottoms?"

*Aw, he likes my designs.* She took a sip of her wine. "I'm glad you asked. So the bottoms were inspired by our tree trimming."

That got an eyelift. "Tinsel?"

"More along the lines of you dancing."

"I seem to recall you were rocking around the tree too."

His face softened, and he placed his hand on her arm, letting it linger. "I had a great time."

His touch launched skittles down her arm. "You can come out now," she called out to her best friend before she did anything stupid and asked Spencer not to move to Italy.

Gwen burst out of the bedroom, wiggling her hips as she danced along the coffee table. "Jingle jammies, jingle jammies, jingle all the way," she sang, shaking her hips in Spencer's direction.

He stood, his expression not giving anything away as he knelt in front of Gwen and ran his hand along the bells. "They jingle, yet soft enough to lounge and sleep in."

Charlie came up beside him. "They're cat toys. Gwen and I practically bought the store out."

"Interesting . . ." He straightened, went over to the couch, and picked up the shirt with the snowflake cookies.

Her heart sank. "You hate it."

"No. Are you kidding?" He tossed the top to Gwen, and she put it on over her tank top, showing off the entire jammies. "I love it, and I want you to unveil this at the Pajama Rama."

"You do?" she asked. Had she heard him right?

"Charlie, this is fun and creative. People will love it. I will take it back to my team, and we'll get it into design and testing." He picked up the Christmas tree pizza top, glancing over at her. "Thank you for showing me what I've been missing."

Her gaze met his again, causing her body to tingle. She placed her hand on her neck. Were they still taking about pajamas?

"Well, I have to get home. My parents are having people over."

"Oh," she said, as Gwen excused herself to change. She reached for her wine. So what that she wasn't invited? No big deal. She needed to clean up anyway. She folded the shirts and put them into his red velvet bag. "Your iPad and sketch kit are both in there too. Jingles seems to have hidden your rubber ball, but I promise I'll bring it to the Pajama Rama."

"Thank you." He didn't seem to be all that disappointed that Jingles had commandeered his ideation ball. "I'll see you tomorrow."

"You're really going to make me give a speech?" she asked, walking him out.

"You're going to be great. Just take a deep breath and picture pointy elf shoes." He chuckled, descending the stairs.

Just then, Jingles flew out the door, pushing Spencer's red ball with her tiny nose in front of Charlie's feet. She called out, "Spencer," as she bent down and snatched the ball from her cat.

He held onto the railing and turned, his blue eyes sparkling as he leaned in. "Yes?"

"Think fast." She tossed his red ball down to him. "You're going to do wonderful things in Italy."

"Thank you, Charlie," he said, catching the ball and disappearing out the door.

She picked up Jingles, cradling her cat in her arms while a stray tear slid down her face. "But I'm going to miss you here."

# Chapter Nineteen

"ALL RIGHT, LADIES in my life. Now that my dad has pumped you with peppermint cocoa, I need those sewing machines revved up, stat." Spencer moved from the fireplace, weaving around his parents' living room that had been set up to pull off a Christmas miracle.

He wanted Charlie to unveil her jammies concept with a beautiful set to pull out of a S.C. bag, and when she did, his family would all waltz into the gymnasium, showing off the Jingle Jammies.

He'd spent all yesterday gathering everything he needed, last night designing the tops, but to pull off the bottoms, he'd needed to enlist some help.

His mom had called around, and in no time set up stations around the house to sew on the jingle bells.

He watched as Dee Dee took the fabric he'd pre-cut, running it through the sewing machine while his mother and Mandy fiddled with theirs.

"I can't believe you're making us sew our pajamas." Kristina came up beside him, her arms full of fabric.

"You want that family holiday photo, don't you?"

"Yes!"

The sound of the doorbell chimes rang through the house. Spencer's heart skipped. It couldn't be Charlie. If it was, he needed to keep her out of here. He headed into the foyer, doing a double take at the familiar face through the glass. He put his finger to his lips.

"Hey, Kristina, can you get the door?" He moved back through the living room.

"Why didn't you do it?" Kristina asked.

"I'm busy ideating." He pulled his red rubber ball out of his pocket and tossed it in the air a couple times, not minding the tiny claw marks that, in fact, were the catalyst for the special top he'd sketched to complement Charlie's jingle bell bottoms.

He stopped in front of the Christmas tree, where Madeline and Ben were playing with the train set. "Hey, we've got a special visitor in the foyer for you two."

Madeline's eyes went wide. "Is it Santa?"

He chuckled at her sweetness. "Better."

They jumped up and raced out of the room, and within seconds, their jubilant screams filled the house.

Pete, it turned out, missed his wife and kids as much as they missed him. Spencer took in his sister's face, all lit up. Maybe they had some things to work out, but what better time to begin than Christmas? "Hey, Pete, you still a large?"

Pete set down his children. "Let's go with an extra-large."

"You got it. Take a seat at an open sewing machine, and

I'll cut the fabric. Kristina will help you make your jammies."

"Jammies," Kristina repeated, cocking her head. "Not pajamas."

He shook his head. "Nope. Nothing but jammies for this fun and festive design."

She gave his arm a playful squeeze. "I always knew you would see things my way."

"Am I doing this right, Spencer?" Mandy asked from across the room, holding up the jingle bells.

"It's perfect. Thanks so much for coming down a day early to help."

"I'm not sure I had much of a choice." She held up her Santa mug. "Although this Grinch hot chocolate was so worth the trip."

He chuckled. His boss's daughter was getting lit off his dad's spiked cocoa.

He took a seat next to her in front of a small card table with an open sewing machine. "So, for tomorrow, the organizer asked if Tye wouldn't mind stopping in, in the afternoon, for a VIP meet and greet. Is that okay?"

She grinned, glancing toward the kitchen where Tye was with Dad, learning his father's secret hot cocoa recipe. "We'd love it."

"And I've got special jammies for both of you that I think you'll like." He reached down and picked up first, the tinsel-inspired pajamas he'd been working on as a backup.

After seeing Charlie's designs, he didn't need the tinsel pair, but Mandy would no doubt love prancing around in them. Maybe in two years or three, they'd make it to the S.C. collection, but not next year.

No, next year was all about the jingle bells.

"How fun!" Mandy admired the red and silver tinsel. "You know, your former college roommate is *never* going to go for it."

"Already thought of that." He reached for the second pair on the sofa, handing them over. "*Star Wars*-themed for your man." He lowered his voice. "I bought this from a competitor."

He turned his attention to the sewing machine. Now all that was left was to make one last pajama set. The one that Charlie would pull out of a Warwick's red satin bag tomorrow night.

The one that he hoped she'd realize was also a one-of-a-kind gift from him to her.

He checked the bobbin and adjusted the throat plate, then eyed his sketch and ran the fabric through the sewing machine. He floored the pedal, and unlike his first night in Brooks Bend, this time, he was in total control.

# Chapter Twenty

"THANK YOU, DAVID," Charlie finished up her call while walking toward the high school. "I will definitely give your offer consideration and let you know next week. Have a merry Christmas."

*I got the job!*

She did a little celebratory jig and entered the building, taking the familiar right and then left turn to the gymnasium. Jillian had called her earlier, demanding that Charlie stop by at two for an impromptu dress rehearsal.

She passed the row of old black lockers and, rounding the corner, was taken aback to see Mandy Warwick Adler in what appeared to be silver pajamas, holding her phone in front of her, flashing shiny red and silver tinsel along the sides of her long bottoms.

"Aren't these the cutest? Don't you feel like dancing?" Mandy continued into the screen, shaking her hips. "The one and only Spencer Carmichael made them for me this week. Let's see the hearts and give him some love, everyone."

Charlie's jaw dropped.

The social influencer spun around, her smile widening.

"Charlie! I was just showing off my jammies to my followers. It's so good to see you again." She came up and gave her hips a shake. "Don't you just love these jammies?"

"It's good to see you." Did she hear that right? Spencer made these pj's? Charlie eyed the silver and red tinsel that made a festive, sparkly fringe on both the top and bottoms.

Had Spencer designed another pair?

Obviously, he had. Her chest tightened as a million questions filled her head. Why did he have her go through all the trouble if he was just going to make his own? Why did he waste her time?

With Mandy staring at her, she lifted her head, not wanting to be rude. "Are you here for the walk-through?"

"No." Mandy shook her head and pointed to the gym. "Tye's in there signing autographs for the VIP event. He's loving every minute with the children." She laughed, adding, "My husband's finally living his best life as Luke Skywalker. I should get in there before he hurts someone with his lightsaber."

Watching Mandy dance her way into the gymnasium, Charlie stood motionless, her thoughts swirling. Why did Spencer announce to all of Brooks Bend that she'd be creating his design if he planned on making his own?

Her heart crashed into her stomach, suffocating all those butterflies. Tonight's speech didn't matter anymore. *He did it because he didn't believe I'd come through.*

"Hey, you."

She spun around to see Spencer behind her in his trademark suit and tie.

"Hi," she said softly, still trying to understand what she'd seen. Had he changed his mind when he said he'd liked her design? She bit down on her lip. Or had he been lying? "Um, can we speak for a minute?"

"Sure." His brow knitted. "Is everything okay?"

She moved toward the lockers, away from the gym's entrance. "I saw Mandy on social media a minute ago showing off the pajamas you made for her."

"She did." He seemed taken aback, but he gave a short laugh. "Well, hopefully, that helped my reputation."

Anger and embarrassment coiled through her veins. *His reputation.* That's what this was about, what these two weeks had only been about. He pretty much said as much shortly after they first met. She shook her head, feeling like the biggest of fools. "Why did you want me to make your pajamas?"

He cocked his head. "What do you mean?"

Her arm went flailing in the direction of the gym. "If you were going to make your own pair and have Mandy unveil them to the world, why waste my time?"

He shoved his hands in his pants pockets. "Charlie, I did make a backup, and I'm sorry I didn't tell you."

*He made a backup.* She folded her arms in front of her. "Because you didn't believe I'd come through? You needed something if I failed."

"Charlie . . ." He reached out to touch her, but she flinched. "It wasn't like that."

"This whole entire week you let me go on thinking I was creating something special, that we were in this together. That I inspired you." Her eyes began to fill. "You led me on."

"Is that what you really think?"

She let out a sigh, glancing down at her overall pants and scuffed work boots. This is who she was—an auto mechanic, not a Fifth Avenue designer. "I'm glad your reputation is rebounding. Have a great life in Italy."

"So that's it? Good-bye. Just like that?"

She nodded and jutted her chin.

"Okay." He closed the distance between them, causing her breath to hitch. He whispered into her ear, "For the record, Charlie Dobbs, you did inspire me and will for a long time to come."

She let out a slow breath as he disappeared down the hall. "This is for the best," she muttered, her eyes watering. Monday, she'd accept David's offer and begin preparing for her new life.

Her throat clenched as reality wrapped around and gave her heart a tight squeeze.

One that wouldn't involve Spencer.

# Chapter Twenty-One

CHARLIE FINISHED READING her favorite chapter and placed the book next to the red poinsettia in front of her mom's grave.

"Merry Christmas, Mom," she said and breathed in the cold air. "You'd be so proud of me." She wrapped her long coat around her. "Your 'scared to open her mouth to a large group' daughter gave not one, but two speeches this holiday season."

Sadness washed over her. For the rest of the day, she'd tried to convince herself that a life with Spencer Carmichael thousands of miles away was for the best.

She couldn't be with a man who didn't believe in her. Who had a backup plan in case she didn't come through.

And now he was gone.

She tightened her coat strap. Soon, he'd be living his best life in Italy and would probably forget he even spent this Christmas in Brooks Bend.

She wiped a tear that had escaped and continued filling in her mom. "I've got some big news. I got a job offer in New York City. Your little girl is moving to the Big Apple.

Can you believe that?"

"Charlie, you got the job!"

She turned to see her dad bundled up in his dark-blue parka, holding a bouquet of pretty red and white roses. He set the flowers down on the grave. "Hi, Lizzy." He patted the headstone. "Merry Christmas, my love."

She smiled over at her dad. "I did get an offer. Earlier today."

"That's great." He stepped back. "Did you accept it?"

She shook her head. "I have until after Christmas to give them my answer."

"You don't seem excited."

"I am." She drove her hands into her coat pockets. "They're offering a great salary, and New York City would be such a new adventure."

"It would." A few seconds went by as they both stared down on her mother's grave. "I'm not going to sell the business."

Her eyes widened at that news delivered so matter-of-factly. "Why not?"

"I'm having too much fun."

"Is that the real reason?" Frustration built up inside her. Was her dad doing to her what Spencer had done this week? Concocted a backup plan behind her back should she fail? "Or are you doing this so I have something to fall back on in case New York doesn't work out?"

"Far from it." Her dad's eyes began to water, and he

pulled out a handkerchief, blowing his nose. "I'm so proud of the woman you've become, Charlie, and your mother would have been too. Barlow Automotive Designs will be lucky to have you, kiddo. I'm looking out for both of us. I'm going to need to keep busy when you move away, and when you're in town, we'll have a place that's ours to get under a hood, install a fuel injector or two, and get our hands dirty."

Her heart warmed, feeling her dad's love. This wasn't what Spencer did—this was her father looking out for his little girl the way he'd always had. "Thank you," she whispered to him and glanced down at the grave. "Thank you both for always believing in me."

He held out his arm. "How about we see where next year takes us?"

She smiled and looped her arm through her dad's. It was time to finally cross Dee Dee's metaphorical bridge and start her new life wherever it led her. "That sounds like a wonderful plan."

"GOOD EVENING, EVERYONE. It's my pleasure to be here for the twelfth day of Elfcapades. Don't we all look festive in our jammies?" Charlie rushed through the high school parking lot, practicing her speech, her cold breath visible in the dark night.

*Don't be nervous.*

She dropped off her coat at the coat check and made her way past the long hallway, saying hellos to many familiar faces, all looking adorable in different-colored jammies. Stepping into the gymnasium, she paused at the entranceway to take in the merriment around her.

And, boy, was it hopping. She hated to say it, but Jillian had pulled off a jolly good time, with a packed dance floor in one corner and what appeared to be reindeer games going on in the other.

In the middle, Tye Adler was high-fiving a group of kids before posing with them for a picture, all five kids wearing festive pj's. Mandy, still sporting the tinsel pajamas, greeted the kids as well.

"Where are your jammies?" Charlie turned to see Gwen in festive red-footie pajamas, her red top displaying the word *Nice* crossed out with a big X.

Charlie dipped her head to her red knit Henley shirt and dark blue jeans. "I can't stay. I'm going to make my speech and leave."

Gwen's eyebrow shot up. "Everything okay?"

"Not really." She didn't want to get into the details in the crowded gymnasium or ruin her friend's fun evening. "I'll tell you about it after Christmas. Maybe we can grab coffee next week."

Just then, Gwen's phone buzzed in her hand. "It's Luke. Let's move out to the hallway, and, yes, we can grab coffee." She raised her phone in the air, and Charlie waved to Gwen's boyfriend, all smiles in his military fatigues.

"You look like you're having fun," he said, blocking the sun out of his eyes.

"I miss you, babe," Gwen said.

"I miss you too. I'll be home next year."

Charlie excused herself to give the couple a chance to catch up, wishing Luke a merry Christmas. She walked down the hall toward the restroom, pushed the door open, and hit the person on the other side. "I'm so sorry."

Jillian emerged in pine-green pajama bottoms with a red top with a huge wreath in the center, passing by without a word.

So much for burying the hatchet at Christmas. Charlie took a step into the restroom.

"Charlie."

"Yes." Charlie held the door open with her back, bracing for the snarky comment coming her way.

"I wanted to apologize for the other night at the Christmas tree lighting. My behavior toward you was appalling."

*Oh.* She moved away from the door, letting it close behind her. This was an unexpected turn of events. "It's okay."

"No, I was really rude, and I know it wasn't the first time." She sighed, raking her fingers through her long, dark hair. "It's been hard following in your footsteps all these months."

*Come again?* "My footsteps," she repeated.

"Evan has such admiration and respect for you. He starts

practically every sentence out with, 'When Charlie and I were together . . .'"

*Wow.* She blinked. *Didn't see that insecurity coming.* Foe or not, she didn't like to see anyone distressed, and especially not at Christmas, and in the middle of the event Jillian had worked so hard to throw. "I think you two are a perfect pair, and everyone can see how he lights up whenever you walk into a room."

"He does?" she asked, her voice cracking.

"Most definitely." She took a deep breath. Jillian was being vulnerable. Maybe she could be too. "I always suspected Evan and I weren't end game. I see that for you both, and I'm happy he found someone that makes him so happy."

"Thank you, Charlie." Jillian's gaze dropped to her footies.

"And . . ." Charlie smiled, hoping she wouldn't regret what she was about to say. But if there was any time to make amends and put away high school pettiness, it was Christmas. "Your Pajama Rama is a hit. Everyone is going to be talking for years about how your twelfth day of Elfcapades was a slam dunk. If you need my help with any post-event activities, I'd be happy to lend a hand."

"I'd love that. I'll call you next week." Jillian excused herself to go find Evan.

*Well, how about that?* Maybe a new friendship would emerge.

"Hey, bestie," Gwen came running up, handing her a red

velvet bag. "It's time."

Her stomach hardened as she took the S.C. bag and made her way to the front. She'd make the speech not because she'd committed to doing it, but because she wanted to prove to herself she could.

When she was done, she'd duck out and head home. Christmas Eve with Jingles, in front of her tree, sounded like a great plan.

She made her way to the stage and took a deep breath as the music stopped and the crowd went silent, all eyes focused on her. Was Spencer in here?

Who cares? *You've got this. Just say what's on the notecard.* She launched into her short welcome, thanking Mandy and Tye, to a round of applause.

She glanced over to the side where Jillian and Evan stood. One tiny improvisation was definitely in order. "I'd also like to thank Jillian Fairweather for all of her work on making this twelfth day of Elfcapades a spectacular success, raising a ton of money for the Children's Hospital, and I think we can all agree it's been a fun way to cap off our twelve days of Christmas kindness. Please join me in giving Jillian a round of applause."

She clapped her hands and smiled in Jillian's direction.

"And now the moment we've all been waiting for." Her confidence grew with each word she delivered without an *uh* or *um*. "Do you all want to see next year's must-have pajamas from The Man with the Bag?" The drum began to roll as she plunged her hand into the red satin bag.

Her eyes went wide. She was not feeling slippery tinsel but soft, tiny, round balls. She pulled out a beautiful pair of red flannel bottoms with jingling bells perfectly sewn into the sides rather than glued with a gun.

And that wasn't it. Her heart melted at the white top: a gray tabby wearing red overalls, a red ribbon curving around the cat like a picture frame.

Her mouth parted, but the words died in her throat. She'd been so wrong. Gwen stepped up next to her, grabbing the bottoms.

"Behold, next year's Jingle Jammies by Spencer Carmichael," she said into the microphone. "Concept design by Charlie Dobbs."

Charlie's shock continued as the whole Carmichael family shimmied into the gymnasium, dancing around in the jammies, all wearing the different Brooks Bend-inspired Elfcapades tops. Kristina twirled Madeline and Ben while Earl dunked Olivia. Even Dee Dee had on a pair, blowing Charlie a kiss.

Just then she caught Spencer standing in the doorway with his own jingle jammies on, sporting the golden goose shirt she'd made. He shot her over a smile but shrank back, disappearing from sight.

Her heart sped up. *Where's he going?*

"Now, let's all hit the dance floor." Gwen put her hand over the microphone, nodding toward the entrance. "What are you waiting for? Go get your fella, already."

Charlie grinned. That's exactly what she was going to do, and she hoped it wasn't too late. She rushed out of the gym and looked right and left, but Spencer was nowhere to be found.

"You'll find him in the town square."

She spun around to see Kristina's warm smile. "He said he was going for a walk to see the Christmas tree lit up one last time before he heads home to Manhattan."

"Thank you." Charlie couldn't help but hug his sister before sprinting down the hallway. She pushed through the glass doors, racing around the corner toward Main Street, picking up her pace through the bitter wind until she reached the town square.

*Where are you?* She stopped, caught her breath, and circled the tree.

Her shoulders slumped as she dropped her head. How could she have been so wrong?

And now he was gone.

She plopped down on a nearby bench, her lips quivering.

"What are you doing out here? You must be freezing."

She looked up to see Spencer closing the distance between them. Her heart began to race, relief washing over her. "I was afraid I missed you."

"I was just taking in the tree from across the street." He pointed all the way to the top. "I think they could have done a better job hanging the lights on those branches. You can barely see them from across the road. What if a gray tabby is looking out the window this very second?"

She laughed, pretty sure Jingles was all snuggled up sound asleep under her tree. "Maybe you could leave that concern in the mayor's suggestion box for next year."

"I'll do that." He slid off his coat and put it around her shoulders before taking a seat on the bench. "How did you think your presentation went? Do you feel good about it?"

"It was a little unexpected." She took a seat next to him. "I'm so sorry I accused you of leading me on."

"I'm the one who needs to apologize. I should have told you what I was doing. It wasn't that I didn't trust you. Far from it." He blew out a breath and took her hand. "I needed to prove to myself that I hadn't lost my creativity. I never would have found it if I hadn't met you."

The electric jolts running through her from his admission forced her up. Maybe it wasn't snowing, but she needed to reveal this minute everything in her heart. "So, I have a few more lines to my presentation. If you have time, I'd love to run them by you."

His lips crooked up, which she'd take as a sign she could start.

She took a deep breath and faced him. "Up until last week, I didn't always have confidence in my abilities beyond a carburetor, but then I met someone who saw something in me that I didn't. I'd also been going through the motions when it came to the holidays these last few years, a hole in my heart for quite some time. Then this man came along and showed me how to perfectly place a tree ornament."

"An important skill," he quipped, draping his arm over the back of the bench.

"And he showed me how to frost a sugar cookie in a way to brighten a face like no other."

He laughed. "I *love* where this is going."

"And he gave me a reason to dance around my tree and have fun again."

He removed his arm from the bench and leaned in.

"You might have believed that I inspired you, but truth is, you, The Man with the Bag, brought Christmas back to me." She took a deep breath, her eyes misting over. "And I know you're going to Italy, and I'm truly happy for you, because I know you're capable of great things, but . . ."

He rose from the bench and stood in front of her, his bright-blue eyes gazing into hers.

"But I hope next year"—she reached over and poked the goose on his chest playfully—"I hope we'll both be right here competing for Brookie."

"I'll make sure of it." He closed the distance between them, placing his finger under her chin and gently lifting it until his lips brushed over hers.

A fireball erupted inside her as he cupped her face and deepened the kiss.

This had to be exactly everything her mother had felt the night she'd revealed to her dad she loved him.

He pulled her into his arms. "You know, a year will go by fast, and Italy's a great place to visit."

"I might not have a lot of vacation time at first." She nestled into his embrace, resting her head on his chest. "I got the job."

"Charlie." He squeezed her arms. "That's fantastic. I knew you'd get it."

"And my dad's not selling the auto shop. I've got a familiar place I can hang out in when New York City seems too big."

"You are going to love Manhattan, trust me." He grew serious, raising an eyebrow. "But I do have an important issue to discuss."

*Oh, no.* "What?" she asked, holding her breath.

"Am I ever"—he wrapped his arms around her—"ever going to get my car back?"

Relief washed over her. "You know German automobiles. I'll see what I can do."

She snaked her arms around his neck. "I can't believe we're really doing this." Yes, it would be tough starting something with this man just as their lives were about to go in opposite directions.

But maybe that was the best time to take a leap of faith.

"The world's your oyster, Charlie Dobbs." Spencer folded his hands over hers. "What do you want this Christmas?"

To say *him* would sound cliché. Still, in his embrace, there was only one thing that would top off this moment and express everything she was feeling for this man perfectly.

"I want it to snow."

# Epilogue

S PENCER WALKED OFF the passenger jet bridge into the airport's terminal and did a spin. After nearly a year in Italy, it was finally great to be home.

He made his way through customs, and an hour later, entered his dark Manhattan apartment, setting his luggage down. The tenant he'd rented it to for nine months had abruptly told him she'd be leaving with only a two-week notice.

He flipped on the lights. *Home sweet home.* It'd been a whirlwind year, but he wouldn't have traded it for anything. The opportunity to work at a huge fashion house in Milan had been everything he'd imagined and more. He was coming home ready to launch his global spring and summer lines of Warwick's first eco-friendly clothing.

He'd also fallen in love with everything the city had to offer, from the food to its culture. He'd be back.

He headed into his kitchen, taking in the numerous Broadway ticket stubs hung up by magnets on the refrigerator door and the scattered shopping bags along his kitchen island, perhaps what was left of Christmas gifts for his tenant's family.

He reached for his phone and gave his mother a call.

"Spencer, how was your flight, dear?"

"Smooth and uneventful. I'm actually feeling invigorated and think I'm going to make my way to Brooks Bend."

"Well, you watch the roads and don't take The Vine."

He couldn't help but smile, recalling the same advice she'd given him last year. Ending the call, he walked into his living room, eyeing the disheveled sofa pillows, blankets strewn all over the place, and scattered magazines on his coffee table.

He shook his head but smiled all the same, picking up the golden goose, who'd had a nice view of Central Park for the last year on his windowsill.

He tapped out the text he'd been planning since he boarded the plane, tugging on the goose's green ribbon. "Brookie, you've got an important job to do tonight."

CHARLIE PULLED UP to the familiar Audi, her breath catching at Spencer leaning against his car's trunk, bundled up in his black coat and red scarf. She turned down the Christmas music and hopped out of her truck. "You just had to take The Vine."

He pushed off the car, closing the distance between them. "What can I say? I wanted to reenact our meet-cute, but then my car died for real." Before she could say something witty, her boyfriend pulled her in for a long kiss.

"You called me the 'tow lady' that night."

He smiled and tugged down her knit hat. "And you left my apartment a mess."

"I have no idea what you're talking about."

"Oh, yes, you do, and what tenant doesn't give her landlord at least a thirty-day notice?" He kissed her nose.

She smirked and wrapped her arms around him, so happy that this moment was finally here. "One who never paid rent, even though she was more than willing and able to do so." She lifted her chin and brushed her lips across his. "And one who was grateful that her boyfriend let her stay in his apartment while he was overseas, but she still missed him every day terribly."

The last year had been challenging, to say the least, but with hundreds of video calls and four visits, they'd made it. Spencer had worked hard on his residency, and she was so proud of him.

And she'd taken the automotive design job, but she knew it wasn't quite what she wanted to be doing when she jumped at the chance this fall to winterize the cars of all of her colleagues. She traded in her heels for her work boots and made her dad an offer to take over the auto shop.

An offer he was pleased to accept. Her father, Dee Dee, and she had celebrated his retirement three weeks ago at the diner, where the two lovebirds had also dropped the big news that they were getting married.

She couldn't be happier for her father and soon-to-be stepmom. Last night they'd all had some fun and trimmed her dad's Christmas tree wearing Spencer's S.C. Jingle Jammies, laughing the entire time.

She grinned over at him. He wasn't supposed to be here until tomorrow, in which they'd invited Mandy and Tye down for Mandy's big reveal of the jammies.

That guest list included Spencer's parents, Kristina and Pete and the kids, Gwen and Luke, and Jillian and Evan.

Yep, Jillian.

The florist had made good on her word to bury the hatchet, and the two had slowly become friends. Jillian even came up to New York City with Gwen and helped Charlie move her things back to Brooks Bend.

"So, do you want me to check out your car?"

He moved out of the way. "Yes, please. I'm just going to get another flashlight out of the back."

"You do that." She gave him a playful side-eye and looked around. None of his tires were trapped in the snow. She got in his car and started the engine. It purred like a kitten. "Spencer, your car's fine." She hopped out and spun around to see him holding Brookie, flashing her a huge grin.

Her mouth flew open. The green ribbon around the goose's neck sported a sparkly diamond ring.

*Oh, my God!* "Yes!"

His eyes crinkled. "May I at least ask the question first?

I've been practicing for eight hours."

She pressed her lips together, nodding.

"I love you so much. Will you marry me, Charlie Dobbs?"

"Yes!" She threw her arms around him and rested her head against his chest, closing her eyes.

Suddenly, something cold and wet touched her cheek.

Her eyes flung open to soft snowflakes falling from the dark sky. Her mother's prophecy finally came true.

*Thank you, Mom.*

She wrapped her arms around his neck, lifting her chin to meet his gaze. "I love you so much, Spencer Carmichael."

He lifted her off the ground and kissed her again as the snow fell around them.

"You know," she said when they finally broke apart. "Just because you're my fiancé, don't think for a second I'm going to go easy on you this week at the Geese-a-Laying Contest. I intend to win Brookie back."

"Challenge accepted." He set the goose in the car before pulling Charlie back into his arms. "Although, if we're living together, Brookie will technically be mine too."

She tugged the ends of his scarf. They'd talked about it a few times over the last couple of months and decided that when he came back from Italy, they'd get a place in Brooks Bend, and he'd commute to the city when he wasn't working from home. "So, what do you want to do this Christmas, Spencer? Build a snowman, make a gingerbread house, sing some Christmas carols, watch *Elf*?"

He laughed and brought her in close as giant white flakes continued to fall from the sky. "I want to spend this Christmas in the snow with you."

## The End

Want more from Robyn Neeley? Check out her sweet romance, *Her Purrfect Match*!

Join Tule Publishing's newsletter for more great reads and weekly deals!

# More books by Robyn Neeley

## The Purrfect Pairs series

Book 1: *Her Purrfect Match*

Book 2: *One Purrfect Summer*

## The Sweet Texas Secrets series

*Sweet Texas Charm*

*Available now at your favorite online retailer!*

# About the Author

Robyn Neeley is an east coast gal who loves to explore super cute small towns; watches way more reality TV than she cares to admit; can't live without Dunkin Donuts coffee; and has never met a Christmas cookie she didn't like. She writes contemporary romance with heart and humor.

Thank you for reading

## Jingle Jammies

If you enjoyed this book, you can find more from all our great authors at TulePublishing.com, or from your favorite online retailer.

TULE
PUBLISHING

Made in United States
North Haven, CT
28 October 2023

43311388R00171